ELLY GRIFFITHS

A GIRL CALLED JUSTICE
THE SMUGGLERS' SECRET

Quercu

QUERCUS CHILDREN'S BOOKS

First published in Great Britain in 2020
by Hodder and Stoughton

1 3 5 7 9 10 8 6 4 2

ISBN 978 1 786 54057 7

Printed and bound in Great Britain by Clays Ltd, Elcograf S.p.A.

The paper and board used in this book
are made from wood from responsible sources.

Quercus Children's Books
An imprint of
Hachette Children's Group
Part of Hodder and Stoughton
Carmelite House
50 Victoria Embankment
London EC4Y 0DZ
An Hachette UK Company
www.hachette.co.uk
www.hachettechildrens.co.uk

For Gabriella and Rafael Brown

HIGHBURY HOUSE

School for the Daughters of Gentlefolk

GROUND FLOOR

KITCHEN GARDEN

SCULLERY

KITCHEN

CORRIDOR

REFECTORY / DINING ROOM

STORE ROOM

COURTYARD

CLASSROOM

CLASSROOMS

MISS DE VERE'S SITTING ROOM

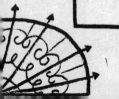

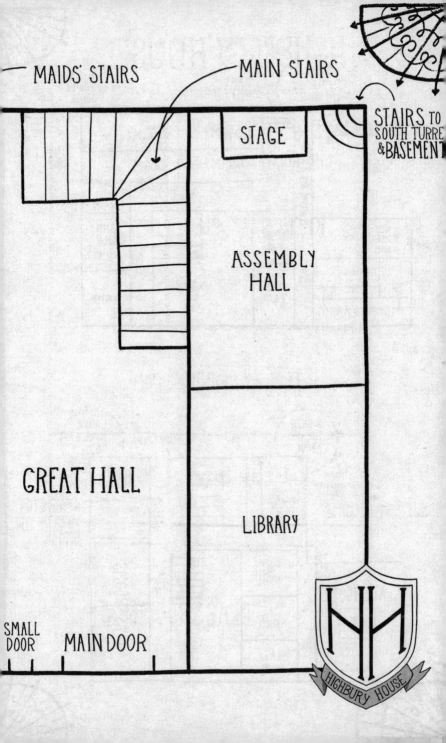

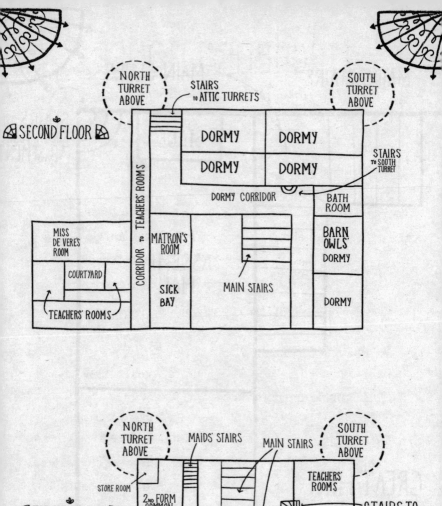

SECOND FLOOR

NORTH TURRET ABOVE

STAIRS TO ATTIC TURRETS

SOUTH TURRET ABOVE

STAIRS TO SOUTH TURRET

CORRIDOR TO TEACHERS' ROOMS

DORMY

DORMY

DORMY

DORMY

DORMY CORRIDOR

BATH ROOM

BARN OWLS' DORMY

MISS DE VERE'S ROOM

MATRON'S ROOM

COURTYARD

TEACHERS' ROOMS

SICK BAY

MAIN STAIRS

DORMY

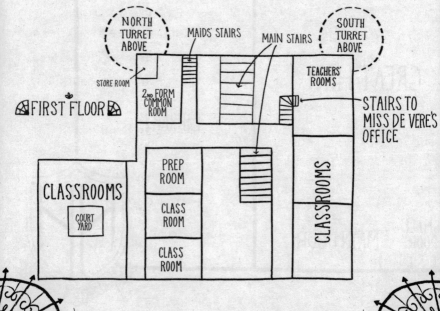

FIRST FLOOR

NORTH TURRET ABOVE

MAIDS' STAIRS

MAIN STAIRS

SOUTH TURRET ABOVE

STORE ROOM

2ND FORM COMMON ROOM

TEACHERS' ROOMS

STAIRS TO MISS DE VERE'S OFFICE

CLASSROOMS

COURTYARD

PREP ROOM

CLASS ROOM

CLASS ROOM

CLASSROOMS

HIGHBURY HOUSE

School for the Daughters of Gentlefolk

Staff

Headmistress	— Miss Dolores de Vere
Deputy Headmistress and Latin Mistress	— Miss Brenda Bathurst
Mathematics Mistress	— Miss Edna Morris
English Mistress	— Miss Susan Crane
History Mistress	— Miss Ada Hunting
Science and Cookery Mistress	— Miss Eloise Loomis
Drama and Elocution Mistress	— Miss Joan Balfour
Music and Geography Mistress	— Miss Myfanwy Evans
French Master	— Monsieur Jean-Maurice Pierre
Games Mistress	— Miss Margaret Heron
Matron	— Miss Maureen Robinson
Housekeeper	— Mrs Jean Hopkirk
Groundsman and Handyman	— Mr Robert Hutchins
Maid	— Dorothy
Scullery maid	— Ada

Form 2 at Highbury House

Form Mistress: Miss Morris

Irene Atkins

Alicia Butterfield

Moira Campbell

Cecilia Delaney

Eva Harris-Brown

Stella Goldman

Joan Kirby

Justice Jones

Flora McDonald

Elizabeth Moore

Freda Saxon-Johnson

Leticia Smith

Susan Smythe

Rose Trevellian-Hayes

Nora Wilkinson

CHAPTER 1

January 1937

The dark shape of Highbury House was getting closer and closer. Justice told herself that she knew the place now – its turrets and spooky ramparts no longer had the power to scare her. But the school was a daunting sight in the twilight, looming up out of the flat marshland, birds – or possibly bats – circling the four towers. There was still snow on the ground here – although, in London, the streets had been clear for weeks. Justice was glad that she had Dad beside her, humming a little tune, his hands relaxed on the steering wheel. It was far better than her first journey to the boarding school, when she'd been alone in a taxi driven by the sinister Nye.

'How are you feeling?' asked Dad, as if he understood.

'All right,' said Justice. 'I'm looking forward to seeing Stella and Dorothy again.'

'Stella's a nice girl,' said Dad. She had visited their house in the Christmas holidays.

'She is,' said Justice. 'She's sometimes a bit reluctant to break school rules though.'

Dad's mouth twitched. 'Try not to break too many rules this term, Justice.'

They were at the school gates, open now but usually firmly closed. The sign on them said, in uncompromising black letters, *Highbury House Boarding School for the Daughters of Gentlefolk*. As they drove slowly along the seemingly endless driveway, they were passed by other cars who had, presumably, already deposited their daughters. A Rolls Royce with a flag on the front that must have belonged to Rose's rich parents, a station wagon driven by a man who looked exactly like Nora – down to his lopsided glasses – and several forgettable cars with identikit parents inside.

Dad parked by the heavy oak doors. Justice got out, holding her overnight bag and shivering a little in the cold air. Hutchins, the handyman, appeared from nowhere to take Justice's trunk. To her surprise, he touched his cap to her and said, 'Welcome back, miss.'

'Thank you,' said Justice. 'Hope you had a good Christmas.'

'Yes, thank you, miss.' Hutchins lumbered away. Dad took Justice's arm and they went through the open doors into the vast hall with its suits of armour and portraits of long-dead members of the Highbury family. A woman in a nurse's uniform was standing by the unlit fire.

'You must be Justice Jones,' she said. 'I'm the new matron, Miss Robinson.'

Justice didn't answer immediately because Miss Robinson was almost the scariest thing she'd seen so far. She was tall and thin with black hair pulled back into a severe bun and she had a prominent nose and chin, like a child's drawing of a witch. Dad raised his hat politely. 'Good afternoon, Miss Robinson. I'm Herbert Jones, Justice's father.'

Miss Robinson inclined her head graciously. 'How do you do, Mr Jones. Justice, do you have your health certificate?'

Justice fumbled in her overnight bag and handed it over. She knew the time had come to say goodbye to Dad and now she found that she just wanted to get it over quickly.

'Bye, Dad,' she said. 'Hope you have some juicy murder trials coming up.' Miss Robinson moved away tactfully. Justice liked her for that.

'Bye, Justice.' Dad kissed her and gave her a quick hug. 'Have a good term. I love you.'

'I love you too,' said Justice. 'Don't forget to send a tuck box.'

She didn't wait to see Dad leave. She went through a door at the back of the hall, up the servants' staircase and along the passageway that led to the dormitories. There was something nice about knowing the way this time. She paused at a door marked *Barnowls*, took a deep breath and pushed it open.

The room seemed to be full of girls all talking at once. 'Isn't she lovely?'

'She's so pretty, like a fairy princess.'

'And she seems so nice. She remembered my name right away. "Hallo, Eva," she said. Just like I was anyone.'

'She knew that I was lacrosse captain. She said we'd have to have a team talk.'

Justice sighed and put her overnight case on the bed. She'd almost been looking forward to seeing the Barnowls again but, now she was actually here, listening to this drivel, she was beginning to have second thoughts. What's more, Stella didn't seem to have arrived yet.

'Have you seen her, Justice?' Eva turned to her, eyes shining.

'Who?' said Justice.

'Miss Heron, the new games mistress. "Hallo, Eva," she said to me—'

'Yes,' said Justice. 'I heard. Amazing. No, I haven't seen her. I've only just arrived. I met the new matron though,' she added.

'Oh, she's ghastly!' said Rose, who was brushing her long blonde hair in the only mirror, which was so high that you had to stand on the bed to see your reflection.

'I liked her,' said Justice. She hadn't really had time to form an opinion but she already found herself wanting to disagree with Rose, partly because Rose herself was always so certain that everyone would follow her lead.

'You would,' said Rose, not turning round from her reflection in the mirror.

'I thought she was scary,' said Nora, adjusting her glasses. 'She looked like a witch.'

'Don't say that.' Eva gave a melodramatic shiver. 'She might put a spell on us.'

'Don't be silly,' said Rose. 'Whoever heard of witches at a boarding school? Buck up, Justice. You don't want to be late for meal. I'm dormy captain again and I can give you an order mark.'

*　　*　　*

Stella didn't arrive until halfway through meal. Justice, who had been trying in vain to eat her food (a junket known to the girls as dead baby), leapt up and called, 'Stella!'

From the prefects' table the Head Girl, Helena Bliss, gave Justice a quelling look. Justice waved at Helena because she knew that this would annoy the older girl, who had a great sense of her own importance.

Stella approached the table, looking tired and rather fed up. She was still in her outdoor clothes and, for a second, seemed almost like a stranger.

'Why haven't you changed?' said Rose, by way of greeting.

'The new matron said it was all right,' said Stella, sitting next to Justice, 'because I was so late.'

'Why are you late anyway?' asked Eva. 'Did you have an accident?'

'My dad's car broke down,' said Stella. 'And we had to walk for miles to find a garage.'

Stella looked as if she wanted to change the subject. Outwardly, she was as calm as ever but Justice could see the signs – a tightening of the jaw and one leg vibrating under the table. Justice knew that Stella's family were poor and that their car was old and unreliable. She thought of Stella and her father walking over the marshes and felt a sudden chill. She remembered the first time she'd seen Romney

Marsh and the note she'd written in her journal: *Chance of escape without being seen: minimal.* They really were isolated at Highbury House – alone on the flat marshland, miles from the nearest village. Last year they had been snowed in with a murderer on the loose. But she had promised Dad she wouldn't dwell on that.

'I'm glad you're here now,' she said. 'I've got a fruit cake in the dormy.'

'Great,' said Stella, who was eating her junket without seeming to taste it. *Probably the best way*, thought Justice. She hadn't yet acquired the knack of swallowing horrible food just for refuelling purposes.

'We can have a feast,' said Eva. 'A Welcome-Home feast.'

Home? thought Justice. School wasn't home. Home was her house in London with the carpets and curtains that had been chosen by Mum, and Justice's room with all her crime novels on the shelves. But, just at that moment, school *did* seem rather homelike, the girls chattering as they ate, lamps lit, the curtains drawn against the night.

'The new games mistress is lovely,' Eva informed Stella.

'She knew that I was lacrosse captain,' said Rose. 'I expect I'll be tennis captain in the summer term,' she added with her usual supreme confidence, probably justified in this case. 'Do you play tennis, Justice?'

'Of course,' said Justice, who had once hit a tennis ball against a wall.

'Spring term is going to be such super fun,' said Eva.

Justice looked round the table. Now all five Barnowls were together: Rose tossing her hair back and admiring her reflection in a spoon; Stella still slightly on edge, chewing her lip as she thought; Nora pushing her glasses further up her nose; Eva beaming around the table.

Perhaps it will be a good term, she thought. She was slightly ashamed of herself for wishing that there would also be a blood-curdling mystery to solve.

CHAPTER 2

The dormitory bell had gone and Justice was walking up the stairs from the second form common room when she heard a loud 'Psst!' Justice grinned as she turned round. Sure enough, Dorothy was hiding behind the red velvet curtain on the top landing.

'Dorothy! There you are!'

'Shh,' said Dorothy. 'Mrs Hopkirk might hear.' Mrs Hopkirk was the housekeeper but Justice had hardly ever seen this mythical creature. All the same, she knew that one of the school's more absurd rules was that pupils must not talk to the maids. So, glancing round quickly, Justice joined Dorothy behind the curtain, which was heavy and musty-smelling, slightly threadbare in places. Dorothy was in her maid's uniform, black with a white apron, and her hair, as usual, looked as if it wanted to escape from its bun. She smiled, rather shyly, at Justice but her hazel eyes were as bright as ever.

'Why didn't you write?' said Justice, lowering her voice, even though the landing seemed to be deserted. 'I wrote you lots of letters.'

'I meant to,' said Dorothy, 'but then my little sister got sick and I had a lot of work to do at home . . .'

Dorothy was the eldest of five children. Justice always envied people with big families (Stella was one of *seven*) but she couldn't quite imagine what it might be like. She hoped that Dorothy's little sister hadn't been seriously ill.

'Which sister?' she said. 'Is she OK now?'

'Elsie, the eight-year-old. Yes, but she's still quite weak. She had a cold and it turned into pneumonia.' Dorothy's voice wobbled slightly.

There had been a maid at Highbury House who had died of pneumonia. Justice could understand why Dorothy had been so worried and the slight resentment she felt about the lack of letters began to fade away.

'I loved getting your letters though,' Dorothy said. 'All about your dad and Peter and the funny man with all the dogs who lives down the road. I read some of it out to my mum and she laughed and laughed.'

Justice was mollified. She'd written pages and pages about Peter, her friend who was studying music, and about her neighbours, including old Mr Altman who had twelve pugs named after the twelve apostles. When Dorothy hadn't answered she had thought that she might have been bored by these outpourings.

'Did you come in to work over the holidays?' asked Justice.

'Of course!' Dorothy looked surprised. 'There's a lot to do before a new term. We have to make all the beds and get the dormies ready. There's food to prepare and the classrooms have to be swept. You wouldn't believe how dusty they get.'

Justice felt rather guilty at this answer. She had never once considered that people would have prepared the school for their arrival. She only thought about how horrible the food was and how uncomfortable the beds, not about the work that had gone into making them ready.

'Did you have to sleep here?' she said. She thought about how spooky the school would feel with only a handful of people in it, all those empty corridors and echoing halls.

'No, thank goodness,' said Dorothy. 'I walked back to the village every night. And I did have Christmas Day and Boxing Day off.'

Dorothy was only three years older than Justice but Justice couldn't imagine only having a few days off a year. She'd spent most of the Christmas holidays lying on her bed reading her mum's books. Mum had written crime novels about a private detective called Leslie Light. They were really good mysteries but Justice often felt sad when she was reading them. Mum had died last year and sometimes, in the books, it was as if you could hear her voice talking to you. She couldn't help feeling slightly jealous of Dorothy, even though she had to work so hard. At least Dorothy had a mother to laugh with.

'Have you seen the new matron?' asked Dorothy.

'Yes,' said Justice. 'She seemed all right. An improvement on the old one.'

'I think there's some mystery about her,' said Dorothy.

Justice felt her heart leap with excitement. Here was a mystery at last. But was Dorothy just imagining things? Matron did look like the villain from a horror story and Dorothy, like Justice, was a big fan of books that featured mysterious villains.

But, before Dorothy could say more, they heard footsteps ascending the stairs.

'I'd better go,' said Dorothy. 'I'm meant to be lighting the fires in the teachers' rooms.'

And she was gone, leaving the curtains billowing in her wake.

The Barnowls' dormy was as cold as ever and the bathroom was positively freezing. Justice's teeth were chattering so much that it was quite hard to brush them. Because it was the spring term she had imagined that Highbury House might be a bit warmer but it was still January and winter lasted longer on Romney Marsh. Justice did a lightning wash and sprinted back down the corridor, planning to get into bed as quickly as possible.

When the other Barnowls were getting ready for bed, Justice managed a few words with Stella.

'Dorothy thinks there's some mystery about the new matron.'

Stella looked at Justice with a familiar expression on her face – half amusement, half apprehension. 'Dorothy always thinks that everything's a mystery.'

'Well, sometimes she's right,' said Justice. 'There was a real murder last term, don't forget.'

'How could I forget?' Stella shivered. 'Let's hope nothing like that ever happens again.'

13

When she was in bed, Justice thought about her friend's words. Stella hadn't enjoyed their adventure last term, although she had been as brave as a lion at the time. Justice hadn't enjoyed it *exactly*. It was terrible that someone had died and there had been moments when she and her friends had been in real danger but, all the same, there had been something very exhilarating about trying to solve the mystery. And she *had* solved it, just in time.

It felt strange, being back in the little iron bed covered with a grey blanket. Strange, but not entirely unpleasant. After Rose had turned the lights out, Justice could hear Stella breathing steadily in the bed next to her. Eva was emitting the regular squeaks that meant that she was already asleep. Justice reached under the bed for the hiding place under the loose floorboard where she had already put her journal, pen and torch. Under the cover of the blanket, she switched on the torch and wrote:

First day back.
    Feels so odd to be here. I was dreading saying goodbye to Dad but, when it came to it, I found that I just wanted to get on with it and be Schoolgirl Justice again.
    Lovely to see Stella and Dorothy. Nora and Eva too.
    Rose is unchanged.
    Dead baby for meal.

Number of times Eva has said 'super': 14
New members of staff: 2
Possible mysteries: 1. The case of the mysterious new matron. (NB: must get details from Dorothy.)

'Justice!' Rose's piercing whisper came across the room. 'You're writing. I can hear your pen scratching. Go to sleep.'

'I will in a minute,' said Justice.

'Perhaps she's writing a love letter to Monsieur Pierre.' Nora was giggling.

'Ah, my leetle cabbage,' Stella imitated the French teacher's voice.

'I will take you away to gay Paree.' Nora again. 'And feed you with snails.'

'Be quiet, all of you,' said Rose. 'Or I'll give you an order mark.'

But it sounded as if she was laughing too.

CHAPTER 3

Last year Justice had arrived three weeks after the start of term and so, as the girls kept telling her, she had missed Miss de Vere's 'welcome back' assembly.

'It's super,' said Eva, helping herself to porridge. 'She always tells us a story and she says things like, "You girls are the future of the human race."'

'The human race is in trouble then,' said Justice. She was feeling rather grumpy. It had been horrible waking up in the cold dormy rather than in her cosy room at home. There had been ice on the inside of the bathroom window and now there was Cook's cement-inspired porridge for breakfast. The porridge had a texture all of its own, rather like quicksand, pulsating and quivering in the saucepan. You were allowed one spoonful of sugar to put on top and this was soon swallowed up by the grey gloop. Justice thought wistfully of breakfasts at home – bread and jam, bacon on Saturdays, sometimes a sausage sandwich at the café in the park.

'She makes announcements too,' said Rose, putting a tiny amount of porridge on her plate. 'Who are the form captains and sports captains, that sort of thing.'

She tossed back her plaits and looked complacent. Rose had been second year sports captain last term and no one doubted that she'd get the call again. Irene had been form captain but this, apparently, changed every term. There were only fifteen girls in the form so, by the end of their time at Highbury, everyone would have had at least one turn. Justice thought that she would probably be in the sixth before she had her chance. Miss de Vere had been fairly nice in her end-of-term report, but Justice thought that her habit of sneaking round the school at night in search of mysteries might count against her when it came to being form captain.

The Barnowls took their seats at their usual table. At the prefects' table, Helena Bliss said, 'Benedictus, benedicat' and then they were allowed to eat.

'Will Helena be Head Girl again?' asked Justice.

Predictable outrage from the Barnowls.

'Of course she will!'

'She's the perfect head girl!'

'She's Head Girl *for life*.' This was Eva, overdoing it as usual. Justice exchanged a glance with Stella. They both knew the head girl wasn't quite as perfect as she seemed. In fact, Helena broke as many school rules as Justice. The difference was that she never seemed to get caught.

After breakfast, they all trooped into the hall for assembly. The girls sat in rows, with the youngest at the front, the sixth formers lounging at the back. All were wearing the school uniform of brown blazer, brown skirt, yellow-and-white striped blouse and long brown socks. The first years looked smart and rather overawed, their blazers slightly too big and their skirts slightly too long. Higher up the school, hemlines were shorter and, although this was against the rules, blouses taken in to show more curvaceous figures. Sixth formers were allowed to wear jumpers instead of blazers and these too seemed suspiciously tight. Justice walked in with the other second years. There were fifteen girls in her class – the five from the Barnowls' dormitory, five Doves and five Robins. Their form teacher was Miss Morris, a stern-looking woman who also taught maths.

The teachers sat in a line on the stage and Justice was able to see the new games mistress, Miss Heron, for the first time. She stood out because, unlike the other teachers, she wasn't wearing a gown and had on what looked like . . . could it be? 'Is that a divided skirt?' she whispered to Eva, who was in front of her.

'I think so,' Eva whispered back. 'Isn't she glamorous?'

Miss Heron was young (for a teacher) and had blonde hair pulled back in a ponytail. She looked around the room coolly but with a hint of a smile. Justice could see why the other girls were so impressed but, for herself, she decided to reserve judgement. 'Don't be dazzled by a witness's demeanour in the box,' Dad always said. 'Wait until you hear what they have to say.'

The new matron, Miss Robinson, sat at the end of the row. *Her* demeanour could not have been more dissimilar. Her arms were folded and she was frowning, dark brows pulled together in a forbidding scowl.

'Isn't she scary?' whispered Eva. 'I hope I don't get ill and get sent to her.'

'Surely you hope you won't get ill anyway,' whispered back Justice. Miss Morris gestured angrily at her to be quiet.

A slightly off-key chord on the piano and Miss Evans, the music teacher, launched into the school song. Justice had never bothered to learn all the words but it was something about 'good times and bad/happy or sad/rain or shine/me and mine'. The writer had obviously had trouble finding a suitable rhyme for 'Highbury House' so it ended with the line, 'O Highbury, your star we see, however far we roam.' It was one of the worst songs Justice had ever heard but the girls sang it with gusto and, before the cacophony had died away, Miss de Vere had glided on to the stage.

The headmistress was a tall, elegant woman who always looked serene and composed. She was wearing an academic gown over a green dress, pale stockings and green leather shoes with a slight heel. The girls all worshipped Miss de Vere, even those who were also slightly afraid of her. Justice wasn't quite sure what she thought. Her father knew Miss de Vere (that was why Justice had been sent to Highbury House) and he both liked and admired her. Justice usually agreed with her father's judgements but she still wasn't quite sure about the headmistress – maybe because she always seemed to know when Justice wasn't quite telling the exact truth.

'Welcome back, girls.' Miss de Vere's voice was low and musical but it reached effortlessly to the back of the hall.

'Welcome to the spring term at Highbury House. Spring is a time of renewal and rebirth. Many of you will recall your mothers spring-cleaning the house at this time of year. Well, we must spring-clean our hearts and our lives.'

Justice stared at the floor. 'Don't think about Mum,' she told herself. 'Don't think about Mum.' It was something she had to remind herself at least once a day. Life was bearable if she didn't compare it to the time when her mother was alive. Not that her mother would have had much time for spring-cleaning. 'Life's too short for dusting' was one of her favourite sayings, as well as, 'A tidy house is a sign of a wasted day.'

'We have several exciting things planned for this term,' Miss de Vere was saying. 'There will be rounders and tennis tournaments and we will be performing a play, an adaptation of *Alice in Wonderland*.'

I bet Helena Bliss will be Alice, thought Justice. All the same, she might have a chance of another part – the caterpillar, maybe, or the white rabbit. In the Nativity play last year she had been stuck with being a narrator.

Miss de Vere then told them a story about three girls who had similar talents for dancing but one didn't work at all and one worked only when it suited her. Only the girl who worked day and night to improve her talent became a famous ballerina. 'Success is one per cent inspiration and ninety-nine per cent perspiration,' said Miss de Vere. 'Ladies might not sweat, but they do perspire.'

The older girls laughed at this. Justice wondered where teachers got stories like these. Was there a book somewhere? *Inspiring Tales for Young Ladies* or *Boring Anecdotes Suitable for Assembly*.

'Now the form captains and sports captains for this term.' Miss de Vere read out the names in a slow, calm voice, ignoring the squeaks of excitement around her. Rose was second year sports captain and Stella was form captain. Justice squeezed her friend's hand, delighted for her.

Miss de Vere ended by reminding everyone that Helena Bliss was Head Girl and everyone clapped dutifully.

'Another exciting innovation this term,' said Miss de Vere, 'is our Good Citizenship programme. I want you girls to become valuable citizens of the world, and that means expanding your horizons beyond this school.'

The girls gazed up at her, not sure what to make of this. Eva could be heard asking what 'innovation' meant.

'I have arranged for our second years and third years to go out into the village and perform good deeds,' said Miss de Vere. 'You will each be assigned a villager – perhaps an elderly person or someone who has been ill – and you will visit them every week to perform useful tasks. I hope that this programme will be of mutual benefit to the school and the local community. *No man is an island.*'

That was said like it was a quotation. Justice made a note to look it up.

'Just one more thing . . .' Miss de Vere looked down on the rows of schoolgirls with a serious expression. 'A reminder that the basement is out of bounds. I know that none of you would dream of going there . . .' Was it Justice's imagination or did the headmistress look in her direction when she said this? Justice and Stella had sneaked into the cellars last year, on the trail of a dead body. 'But just to make it clear, anyone caught in the lower regions of the school will be in serious danger of expulsion. Have a good and productive day, girls. School dismissed.'

'I don't like it,' said Rose. 'What if we have to go into a horrible smelly house and clean it for them?'

It was recess and the girls were walking round the courtyard, trying to keep warm. This daily activity always reminded Justice of pictures of convicts exercising in prison.

'I think it'll be fun,' said Justice. 'And it'll get us out of school.'

'I don't want to get out of school,' said Rose. 'Some of us have lacrosse practice to do.'

Justice hated lacrosse, the school's number one sport, and she had a feeling that lacrosse hated her right back. Rose was very good at it though.

'Why do we have to do the citizen thing?' whined Eva, who was walking with Nora, both of them with heads bowed against the wind. 'Why not the other forms?'

'I heard Miss Morris say it was because the second and third years don't have exams to prepare for,' said Stella. 'And Miss de Vere thinks it's important to form our characters when young.'

This last was said in what was clearly meant to be Miss de Vere's voice, deep and soulful. The girls all laughed. But Justice wondered if there was something more behind the Good Citizenship Programme than met the eye. And why was Miss de Vere so keen to stop them going into the basement? Justice put her hand in her pocket and her fingers closed on a folded note. It was from Dorothy.

Have found out something about the new matron.
Meet me in my room at midnight.
D

CHAPTER 4

Justice was used to midnight meetings. Dorothy always specified this time; she loved horror stories where everything happened at 'the witching hour'. And it was easy to believe in that sort of thing at Highbury House. When Justice looked out of the window before bedtime, she could see the tower, dark against the moonlit snow. The old tower in the grounds was meant to be haunted by a girl who had died in there, imprisoned years ago by a tyrannical father. Even now, it was easy to picture a white face looking out at you, or imagine that the wind howling in the trees was actually the sound of Grace Highbury, sobbing in anguish. Luckily Justice was too sensible for such flights of fancy, she told herself. She got into bed and rubbed her feet together to get them warm. Then she wrote in her journal:

First day back was as good as could be expected. The famous assembly was boring apart from the news about the school play. I'd love to be in Alice! And at least this Good Citizenship thing will give us a chance to escape from Dracula's castle sometimes. All the girls think Miss Heron is wonderful because she wears divided skirts. I'm not so sure myself. I will keep her under observation. D thinks there's some mystery about the new matron. I'll find out more tonight.
Also: why did Miss DV say that the basement is out of bounds? Hasn't it always been out of bounds? Is this another mystery???

Rose was telling her to stop writing, so Justice closed her journal and, when the lights went out, slipped it into its hiding place under the floorboards. Then she lay in the dark and tried to keep awake. The trouble was that she was tired after her first full day back at school. Her eyes kept closing, so she sat upright, hoping that the cold air would stop her feeling sleepy. As usual, she recited old murder trials in her head:

Rex v Stanley

Rex v Donagh and West
Rex v Hamilton
Rex v Pewsey . . .

It was no good. Her head kept dropping on to her chest. She sat up even straighter and listened to the night sounds; Eva squeaking, Rose muttering in her sleep, the old floorboards creaking, a fox calling from the grounds. Justice looked at her watch. Eleven o'clock. She would have to go now. If she stayed in bed any longer she would fall asleep and she wanted to find out what Dorothy knew about the new matron.

Justice climbed out of bed and felt for her slippers, then she eased on her heavy, wool dressing gown, which she had put over the end of her bed instead of hanging it up. Eva gave a louder than usual squeak and Justice held her breath, but no one woke up. In fact, the noise seemed to have sent Eva into a deeper sleep and the room was quiet. Justice tiptoed to the door.

She crept along the corridor, avoiding the places where she knew there were loose floorboards. The danger lay beyond the green baize door – Matron's room was on the other side. The previous matron always seemed to be sneaking about at night. Miss Robinson had made her evening rounds at nine o'clock, pacing the corridor in shoes so heavy that you could hear her coming a mile off. Justice hoped that the new matron was now tucked up in bed with a good book.

Justice paused on the landing. No sound except for the grandfather clock ticking two floors below. She sprinted for the staircase that led to the servants' quarters. Actually, Dorothy was the only person who slept in the attic now. Cook and Mrs Hopkirk had more comfortable rooms on the ground floor and the other maids came in from the village. A minute later, Justice was tapping on Dorothy's door.

'It's not midnight yet.' Dorothy pulled her into the room.

'I couldn't stay awake.'

Dorothy's room was large and bare. The only pieces of furniture were an iron bed with a table beside it and a large wardrobe. Mary's bed had been taken away after she died last year. Justice thought of Mary with a sudden pang, although she'd never met her. Mary had died here, miles away from her family and friends, and no one but Dorothy seemed to mourn her. Justice didn't say this to Dorothy though. At least there was a patchwork quilt on Dorothy's bed, which made the room look more cheerful, and Justice secretly envied Dorothy the teddy bear that sat on her pillow. Dorothy was three years older than Justice and much more grown-up in many ways, but she wasn't scared to be childish too. Pupils were allowed 'one keepsake from home' but Justice would have been embarrassed to bring a toy. She had her survival kit (journal, pen, torch and penknife) instead.

Now they sat on the bed and pulled the cover over them. It was very cold in the attic. The roof was high with a tiny, curtainless window in the rafters. Justice could still hear the wind howling across the marsh, rattling the glass pane. All the same, she felt a warm glow inside that came from being with her friend. She realised how much she had missed Dorothy.

'So,' she said. 'What's all this about Matron?'

'Well,' Dorothy settled herself against the pillows. Like Nora, she loved telling stories. 'Do you know Ada, the scullery maid?'

'No.'

'Really?' Dorothy was always amazed at how little Justice and the other girls knew about the maids who did all of the work around the school. 'Well, this morning Ada was feeding the pigs and she slipped on the ice outside their sty. Ada's ankle was all blue and swollen, so Cook told her to go to Matron. She could hardly walk, so I helped her. Miss Robinson looked at Ada's ankle and told her that it was only sprained and to put a cold compress on it.

31

An hour later, Ada was still in agony so Hutchins drove her to the hospital. Her ankle was broken.'

'Poor Ada.'

'Yes, and her family really need her wages. They can't afford a doctor, either. Anyway, the point is that Miss Robinson – who's supposed to be a nurse – didn't recognise a broken ankle. Hutchins says you could practically see the bone sticking out.'

'Yuck.' Justice was very squeamish for someone who wanted to be a detective.

'I'm sure there's a mystery about Miss Robinson,' said Dorothy. 'She really didn't seem to know what to do about Ada's ankle.'

'Do you think she isn't actually a nurse at all?' Justice could feel her spirits rising at the thought of doing some investigating. 'Do you need to be a nurse to be a school matron?'

'You need to be able to recognise a broken ankle,' said Dorothy. 'And she wears a nurse's uniform.'

'That doesn't mean anything,' said Justice. 'Anyone can buy a uniform.'

'But why would someone pretend to be a matron?'

'That's what we have to find out,' said Justice. 'We might have to follow Miss Robinson. There's a mystery about the basement too. This might turn out to be quite an exciting term, after all.'

'Miss Robinson looks sinister too,' said Dorothy.

'My father says that it's the innocent-looking people you have to look out for,' said Justice.

Dorothy dismissed Herbert Jones QC with a wave of her hand. 'Mrs Hopkirk, the housekeeper, says that some people have the mark of the devil. I think Miss Robinson has it.'

'What do you think of Miss Heron, the new games mistress?'

'Oh, she seems ever so nice. She gave me a lovely smile when I lit the fire in her room.'

Justice gave up. 'Have you heard we're going to be allowed to go to the village?' she said. 'It's part of some citizenship idea. It'll be great to escape from school for an afternoon.'

'You might see my house,' said Dorothy, excitedly. 'It's Rectory Lane, number ten, the last cottage before you get to the green.'

'I wish I could go in and meet your family,' said Justice. 'John, Susan, Elsie and baby Tommy.'

'I wish you could too,' said Dorothy. 'Mother would love to see you. I've talked about you lots at home. Do you know where you'll be going?'

'No. Miss de Vere is going to assign us to different people.'

'As long as you don't go to Smugglers' Lodge.'

The name intrigued Justice. 'Where's that?'

'It's the big house down by the shore. It's meant to be haunted by sailors who drowned. The wreckers used to shine lights so that boats would hit the rocks and get shipwrecked. Then they'd steal everything that was on board. People say that sometimes, late at night, you can still see strange lights in Smugglers' Lodge.'

'Who lives there now?'

'Just an old man and his housekeeper. He keeps himself to himself, Mum says.'

'Doesn't sound like any of us will be sent there. Shame really. I bet there's some mystery about the house.' Far below, the clock chimed midnight. 'I'd better go,' said Justice.

'Don't forget to keep an eye on Matron.'

'I will,' said Justice, more to please Dorothy than because she thought there was anything in her suspicions.

She descended the stairs and had just begun to open the door to the landing when she heard another door open. Matron's room. Justice pushed gently so that she could see through the gap. Miss Robinson was standing by the entrance to the dormies. She was holding a large torch and looked as if she was listening. Justice held her breath. After a few minutes, Miss Robinson set off in the direction of the main staircase. Her feet made no sound as she passed.

Justice counted to ten then shot out of the door, ran across the landing and hared down the dormy corridor, not bothering about the creaky floorboards. When she was safely in bed, she wrote in her journal:

Miss Robinson couldn't recognise a broken ankle. Query: is she even a real nurse?

What was Miss Robinson doing out of bed at midnight?

And why was she wearing gym shoes?

CHAPTER 5

The next morning, the second year form mistress read out their Good Citizenship assignments. The girls were to travel into the village on Wednesday afternoon, which was usually kept free for activities.

'Will we go in Hutchins's car?' asked Eva.

'No,' said Miss Morris, pushing her glasses up over her short, pale hair. 'Use your common sense, Eva. How would thirty girls fit into one car? You will walk there. It's only half an hour's walk if you move briskly. Miss Heron will accompany you.'

Some of the girls looked excited at this news. Justice had mixed feelings. She was keen to escape from school for an afternoon, but she didn't fancy half an hour's brisk walk with all the second and third years, accompanied by Miss Heron blowing her whistle at them.

Miss Morris read their names in alphabetical order.

'Irene Atkins. You're to go to Mrs Bates, a mother with three young children. Alicia Butterfield, you're assigned to Mr Jenkins, an elderly man who needs help writing letters.'

Stella was assigned a Mrs Graham, who had four children. 'Just like home,' she whispered to Justice. Eva was the envy of the class because she got an elderly woman who wanted her dog walked. Eventually Miss Morris got to J.

'Justice Jones. You are to visit Mr Arthur. I don't know what kind of help he needs. Presumably he's elderly and infirm. An able-bodied man wouldn't be part of the programme.'

'Where does Mr Arthur live?' asked Justice. She wondered if his house was close to Dorothy's. 'Please, Miss Morris,' she added, seeing the teacher's face.

'I don't believe I asked for questions, Justice,' said Miss Morris. Then, relenting slightly, 'He lives in a house called Smugglers' Lodge. It sounds most picturesque. Now, Joan Kirby . . .'

*　　*　　*

Their first lesson that morning was games. Justice hated sport. She was one of the only girls in the class not to be in the lacrosse team and Rose frequently called her a 'rabbit', an insult reserved for anyone who couldn't throw or catch. But at least the walk to the gymnasium gave her the chance to talk to Stella. As they skirted the lacrosse pitch, Justice managed to slow Stella down so that they were out of earshot of the other girls.

'I went to see Dorothy last night,' she said.

'You got out of bed after lights out?' Stella looked half disapproving, half amused. 'I thought you said you weren't going to break any school rules this year.'

'Did I say that? Well, Dorothy thinks there's some mystery about the new matron.' She told Stella the story of Ada's ankle.

'That might not mean anything,' said Stella. 'My mother was a nurse during the war and she said that even doctors often got things wrong.'

'It's a bit suspicious though,' said Justice. 'And I saw Miss Robinson sneaking around at midnight.'

'Sneaking around? What do you mean?'

'She was wearing gym shoes so she wouldn't be heard. And she was carrying a torch.'

'What was she doing?'

'I don't know – but I'm going to keep an eye on her. Oh, and Dorothy told me that Smugglers' Lodge was haunted.'

'The place where you're going to be a Good Citizen?'

'That's right. Maybe I'll end up reading to a ghost or taking a werewolf for a walk.' Justice pulled a face.

'Hurry up, girls. No time for talking.'

Miss Heron was standing by the gymnasium with a stopwatch in her hand. She was wearing a cricket jumper and the shockingly modern divided skirt. The drained swimming pool was behind her, now covered with a tarpaulin.

'Hurry up and get changed,' Miss Heron told the second form, who were standing around, stamping their feet to keep warm.

'Please, Miss Heron,' said Rose, 'are we going to play lacrosse?'

'No,' said Miss Heron, 'we're going on a cross-country run.'

Some of the girls groaned. Justice and Stella exchanged looks. In Justice's opinion, almost anything was better than lacrosse – but running round a freezing field in January? It wasn't high on her 'must do' list. But she went indoors and changed into her gym kit: aertex top, skirt, long socks and sports shoes. When she got back outside it seemed colder than ever.

'Cross-country running builds stamina and it's good for your mind and body,' Miss Heron told them. 'It's also about tactics. The race is not always about being the swiftest. Pace yourself and don't run too fast at first. Round the field, past the spinney and the tower and back. Twice.'

Some of the girls started to protest that it was too far, but Miss Heron blew her whistle while they were still talking.

Despite Miss Heron's warning, Rose went off like a rocket, followed by Alicia and a few of the sportier girls. Stella was in the group just behind them. Justice set off as slowly as she dared and was soon at the back of the group.

The field seemed miles long. Justice had a stitch before she'd even reached the spinney, a group of trees surrounding the tower. In the daylight the tower looked innocent enough but, having been locked in there by a distinctly human villain last year, Justice still viewed the building with a certain amount of wariness.

At least thinking about villains had taken Justice's mind off her stitch. As she reached the trees she passed several other girls who had started too fast and had now stopped, red-faced and breathless.

'Come on, girls. Keep going.' Justice jumped. She hadn't realised that Miss Heron was running beside them. Ponytail flying in the wind, the games mistress did not even seem out of breath. 'Good work, Justice,' said Miss Heron. 'You're pacing yourself well.'

Justice kept going. She was amazed that Miss Heron even knew her name. The previous games teacher had treated her with utter disdain.

It was quite fun running through the trees, although the runners in front had stirred up the mud and soon Justice's face was spattered. When they rounded the spinney though, it was uphill back to the top of the field and several girls stopped again. Justice passed Nora and Eva, holding on to each other for support. Nora's glasses were covered in mud and Eva was almost in tears.

Justice ran on, reciting murder trials in her head to take her mind off her aching legs. Soon she caught up with Stella.

'This is torture,' panted Stella, who was normally good at games.

'Torture,' agreed Justice. But, to her surprise, she was almost enjoying it.

'No talking,' shouted Miss Heron, just behind them. 'Use your breath for running.'

Round the field again. Down into the spinney. Now Justice had left Stella behind and there were only three girls ahead of her. One of them was Rose. Justice could see her blonde plaits flying as she ran through the trees. The others were Alicia and Moira, a red-haired Scots girl who excelled at lacrosse and swimming.

Murder trials got Justice past the Tower and on to the long uphill path to the finish line. Rose had stopped to catch her breath but, when she saw Justice gaining on her, she started running again. Moira was a long way in front now and it looked as if Alicia would be second. The race for third place was between Rose and Justice. Justice tried to focus, to concentrate on putting one foot in front of the other. She looked ahead, to the top of the hill where Miss Heron was waving at them, and not at Rose, who was jogging beside her. Justice had always thought that she despised competitive sport but suddenly she wanted to beat Rose more than anything on earth.

'Come on, Justice,' shouted Miss Heron. 'Dig deeper.'

Justice channelled all of her willpower into her tired legs. She remembered all of the times when she'd wanted to give up but hadn't, all the times when she'd fought against missing Mum, all the times when she'd had to strike out on her own, despite being scared or uncertain. Suddenly she found that she was going faster, almost as if someone was pushing her from behind. She knew that she was ahead of Rose. Only a few more steps. The next thing she knew was Miss Heron patting her on the back. 'Third place. Well done, Justice.'

Justice collapsed on to the ground, the blood singing in her ears. She had come third. Out of all the class, she had been in the top three. She had beaten Rose.

It felt like the happiest moment she had ever known at Highbury House.

CHAPTER 6

On Wednesday afternoon the second and third years walked into the village for the Good Citizenship afternoon. They were accompanied by Miss Heron, dressed as ever in her divided skirt. It was a sunny day but the wind was strong and the first part of the walk, following the road across the mashes, was hard-going. The girls wore their gaberdines and walked in single file, bent almost double. Eventually they reached the crossroads and Miss Heron pointed the way to the village. 'There's a footpath over that stile,' she said. 'It'll be nicer than following the road.'

It *was* a lot nicer – they were sheltered by trees and hedges and were able to walk normally. Miss Heron began singing marching songs and soon they were all joining in, swinging along through the grey winter fields, their breath billowing around them.

'I wonder where Miss Heron is from,' Justice whispered to Stella while everyone was chanting 'Left, left, I had a good job and I left.' 'She seems to know the countryside round here very well.'

'Who knows? I'm just glad to be out of the wind,' said Stella. 'My ears have gone numb.' They all had their school hats jammed as low as they could go but they weren't much protection. Justice wished she had a cap like her friend Peter's, which had flaps over the ears but, of course, Highbury House girls were not allowed to wear anything so useful.

Before long they could see the spire of the village church and then the thatched roofs of the houses. At the village green, Miss Heron stopped and consulted her list.

'When I call your name, you're to go and find the house where you'll be doing your Good Citizen duty. You've all got a map and the addresses. We are meeting back here at four-thirty. Does everyone have a watch?'

Eva said that hers only worked sometimes.

'Make sure it works today,' said Miss Heron briskly. 'It's half past two now. Off you go. Justice, wait a minute.'

Justice waited. She hoped Miss Heron wouldn't keep her for long. She'd looked at the map and seen that Smugglers' Lodge was a little way out of the village, right on the edge of the sea. She would have to allow another ten minutes' walk. She felt slightly nervous at the thought of visiting the supposedly haunted house, but a larger part of her felt intrigued. Besides, in her experience, saying that a place is haunted is often a ruse to stop people going there.

'You did well in cross-country yesterday, Justice,' said Miss Heron.

'Thank you,' said Justice. 'I quite enjoyed it.'

Miss Heron laughed. 'I knew you'd be a good runner as soon as I saw you.'

'Really?' said Justice. 'But I'm terrible at games. You ask anyone.'

'It's not about being good at games,' said Miss Heron. 'It's about being determined.'

Well, Justice knew all about being determined. She wondered if that was all the teacher had to say to her.

'I'm putting together a cross-country team,' said Miss Heron. 'Unless I'm much mistaken, you'll be part of it.'

Justice could hardly believe her ears. Being on a sports team at Highbury House meant that you were Someone. You got to miss lessons and sometimes had extra food at tea.

Justice never thought that she would be one of these elite creatures. It was an odd thought. She had always seen herself as an outsider at Highbury House but, if she got on a team, she would be One of Them. She wasn't sure that she liked the idea, much as she appreciated the praise. Then she remembered how much she'd enjoyed beating Rose in the race.

'Can you have girls' cross-country teams?' she asked.

'Oh, yes,' said Miss Heron. 'One day women will even run marathons.'

Justice remembered Mum telling her about a man in Ancient Greece who ran twenty-six miles from Marathon to Athens with a message about a battle. The race was named after this feat, but Justice seemed to remember that the messenger had died as soon as he delivered his news. She was pretty sure that running twenty-six miles would have the same effect on her.

'Can I go, miss?' she asked. 'I think it's quite a long walk to Smugglers' Lodge.'

'I'll go with you,' said Miss Heron, unexpectedly. 'I'd like to see the place for myself.'

As they walked through the High Street – which possessed only one shop, a depressed-looking tea shop and a pub called The Galleon – they could see girls in brown coats knocking on doors. Justice watched Eva being welcomed by an old lady and a very excited-looking spaniel. She wished that she was calling on one of these cosy-looking cottages instead of a haunted house. Where was Rectory Lane? she wondered. It would be good to see Dorothy's house. Maybe she could even visit one day.

They reached the end of the street and crossed the coast road. And there, in front of them, was nothingness, just grey shingle and grey sky. It took Justice a few minutes to realise that she was actually on the beach. The stones had formed a bank and it wasn't until they reached the top of this that they could see the sea itself, a darker grey than the sky and flecked with white waves. The seagulls were flying low over the water, calling in their eerie, echoing voices. The wind was stronger here and it brought with it a harsh, briny smell that made Justice's eyes sting.

'Breathe it in,' said Miss Heron. 'Sea air is very good for your lungs.' She stretched out her arms and raised her face to the sky.

Justice looked around. There was only one house on this side of the road – a large white building with a grey roof and a tower at one end. It looked bleak and somehow threatening, as if it was waiting for something. The windows looked blankly out to sea but, as Justice watched, the low afternoon sun flashed against the glass – once, twice, three times. It was like a message in Morse code. *Save Our Souls.*

'Is that Smugglers' Lodge?' she asked. She thought she knew the answer.

Miss Heron opened her eyes. 'I think it must be,' she said. 'What a curious house. Odd to build it so close to the sea.'

'Someone told me that it was haunted,' said Justice.

'Oh, there are always stories about old buildings,' said Miss Heron. 'I wouldn't worry about it. I'm sure you'll have an interesting and enjoyable time. See you on the village green at four-thirty.'

Don't go, Justice begged her silently. But the teacher headed away, walking surprisingly fast over the stones.

The only way to reach the house was across the beach itself. Justice stumbled over the sliding pebbles. The house seemed to be getting further away than ever. The sun had gone in and the wind was driving in from the sea. As she approached, she could hear the deep bark of a dog. Maybe she was going to be a dog-walker, like Eva? Well, that wouldn't be too bad. She reached the house, which was raised on a slight bank, and climbed the steps to the front door. The walls looked even higher from this angle, their white paint peeling and weather-beaten in places. The door seemed unusually high too, and it was black with a brass knocker in the shape of an anchor. Justice took a deep breath and knocked boldly.

Another bark, loud and clear like a warning. Then the door was opened by a tall woman with iron-grey hair. She looked almost as terrifying as Miss Robinson but she gave Justice a friendly smile and said, 'Justice Jones? I'm the housekeeper, Mrs Kent. Mr Arthur is expecting you. Are you cold? Would you like some hot chocolate?'

'Yes, please,' said Justice. Her spirits were rising. They sometimes had cocoa at school for a treat, but it was thin and watery, nothing like proper hot chocolate.

Mrs Kent led her into a room dominated by a huge window that seemed to be full of the sea. A large dog – *an Alsatian*, Justice thought – was sitting by the door. He wagged his tail when he saw Justice but didn't move towards her. Justice thought about her neighbour, Mr Altman, and his dogs. The pugs always ran to greet any visitor, yapping and snuffling, but this seemed an aloof and superior animal.

A man was sitting in an armchair by the window.

'Mr Arthur?' said Mrs Kent. 'Justice is here.'

The man turned and smiled but he didn't quite look in their direction. The dog came to his side and Mr Arthur felt for his collar and stood up slowly. It was only then that Justice realised that Mr Arthur was blind.

'Welcome, Justice,' he was saying. 'Come and sit down. Mrs Kent will get you something to drink.'

'I'm making hot chocolate,' said the housekeeper. 'Would you like some, sir?'

'That would be delicious,' said Mr Arthur.

Justice sat opposite him. Mr Arthur wasn't that old, she realised, probably only in his late fifties or early sixties. She wasn't good at adult ages; the teachers at the school all seemed about a hundred, for example, while her dad remained perpetually young. But Mr Arthur's hair was grey, not white, and his face was not particularly lined. He had a scar over one eye, though, and the skin was puckered around it. He must have guessed that she was looking at this because he said, 'I was injured in the war. I was a pilot and my plane caught on fire. I was lucky not to die – but I was left completely blind.'

'I'm sorry,' was all Justice could think of saying.

'That's all right,' said Mr Arthur. 'I've got Sabre here to help me.' He patted the dog, who was watching him intently, as if trying to guess what his master's next need would be.

'He's beautiful,' said Justice. Then she stopped. Was it

bad to comment on how things looked to someone who couldn't see?

But Mr Arthur just smiled. 'He is, isn't he?'

Mrs Kent brought in the hot chocolate and slabs of fruit cake on a tray. The chocolate had real cream on the top and the cake was delicious. Justice was always hungry when she was at school so she had to stop herself wolfing it down in two bites.

Mr Arthur took a delicate sip of his drink. 'The reason I wanted you to come,' he said, 'was to help me with the newspapers. I like to keep up-to-date on world affairs but Mrs Kent has better things to do than read to me. I thought that, if you could come and read the newspapers to me once a week, it might be a pleasant way to pass the time. What do you think?'

Justice swallowed down some cake. 'I think it would be very nice,' she said. She meant it too. Sitting in a warm room eating cake and reading the papers was far better than looking after babies or even walking dogs. *So what if the house is haunted*, she told herself, *at least I can drink hot chocolate every week*. But she couldn't suppress a tiny twinge of fear at the thought of the drowned sailors and the ghostly lights in the tower at night.

On a table nearby was about a week's worth of *The Times*.

Justice picked the one with the most recent date.

'Shall I start reading?' she asked.

'Please do.' Mr Arthur turned in her direction, although his eyes still looked past her. Sabre, on the other hand, watched her intently.

The news was mainly about communists going on trial in Russia, accused of plotting to kill Stalin. Justice struggled to pronounce the names but Mr Arthur nodded as if he understood. She could have sworn that Sabre nodded too. There was also something about the King's coronation in May and about a man in America who was apparently building a flying car. Mr Arthur was very interested in this article and asked Justice to read it again.

'Would you like to fly in a car, Justice?' asked Mr Arthur.

'I don't know,' said Justice. 'My dad drives very fast – over thirty miles an hour sometimes. That feels a bit like flying.'

'Your father was a pilot in the war, wasn't he?'

'Yes,' said Justice. 'How did you . . .' She was going to ask how he knew but realised that this might sound rude.

'My dad was in the Royal Flying Corps,' she said, 'but he doesn't talk about it much. He's a lawyer now.'

'Herbert Jones QC,' said Mr Arthur. 'I know.'

He looked as if he was about to say more but, at that

moment, Mrs Kent appeared in the doorway. 'It's twenty past four,' she said. 'What time do you need to be back, Justice?'

'Half past,' said Justice. She stood up. 'I have to go. Sorry.' She was amazed at how quickly the time had gone. The window was almost black.

'See you next week,' said Mr Arthur. He smiled but his head was turned away. Sabre uttered a single staccato bark which might well have been 'Bye.'

It seemed very dark outside. Justice couldn't see the sea but she could hear it, crashing against the bank of stones. How close did it come to the house, she wondered. Looking back, she could see lights in the windows of Smugglers' Lodge and one shining in the tower, very high up. She remembered Dorothy's story about the lights that had lured the sailors to their death. She hurried over the pebbles, trying to keep her eyes on the village and safety.

She was the last to arrive at the green but Miss Heron just ticked her name off the list and said nothing. Then they set off, sticking to the road this time.

'What was yours like?' Justice asked Stella.

'OK,' said Stella. 'The children wanted to play hospitals and I had to be the patient. The littlest one drew spots all over my face. I don't think I've wiped them all off. What about you?'

'I don't know,' said Justice. 'Mr Arthur is blind and he wants me to read the newspapers to him.'

'Well, that sounds quite easy.'

'Yes,' said Justice. She thought about her visit. She had liked Mr Arthur and Mrs Kent (and Sabre) but there was still something odd about the house on the edge of the shore. She thought about the single light shining in the tower.

'Dorothy says that the house is haunted,' she said.

Stella laughed. 'Dorothy thinks everywhere is haunted. Come on, let's catch up with the others. I can't wait to get back and have something to eat.'

That night Justice wrote in her journal:

Things to discover:
  Is Miss Robinson a real nurse?
  How does Miss Heron know the countryside so well?
  How does Mr Arthur know about Dad?
  Is Smugglers' Lodge haunted or is there some other mystery?

CHAPTER 7

The next morning, in form time, Miss Morris went around asking the girls about their Good Citizenship experiences.

'I enjoyed it,' Justice told her firmly. 'I liked Mr Arthur. He had a gorgeous dog too. An Alsatian.'

'Well, don't pat the creature unless you're allowed to,' said Miss Morris. 'Guide dogs are working animals, not pets. I'm glad you enjoyed your assignment though.' She turned to move on to Stella at the next desk.

'Miss Morris?'

The teacher turned, eyebrows raised.

'Miss Morris,' said Justice. 'How did we get our assignments? I mean, who chose which house we went to?'

'Miss de Vere organised the whole thing,' said Miss Morris, in her most quelling voice. 'Now get on with your silent reading.'

The first lesson that morning was games and, once again, Miss Heron made them run round the field and the spinney twice. Justice tried the same tactics again, starting slowly and gradually moving through the field. This time she was even more successful, coming second to Moira. Rose was third and Alicia fourth. Alicia was Rose's best friend and Justice wondered whether she had let Rose beat her. All the same, Justice felt wonderful. Even as she doubled over, trying to get her breath back, she felt a hundred feet tall. She had come second. She, Justice Jones, who was the worst in the class at sport.

'Moira, Justice, Rose and Alicia,' said Miss Heron, 'you four are my cross-country team. The reserve will be . . .' She looked around at the other girls, who were either lying on the ground or bent double, panting. 'Stella,' she said. Justice grinned broadly and Rose gave her a sour look. 'We will meet for extra runs at the weekends and after school when the evenings get lighter,' said Miss Heron. 'I hope to be able to enter us for a competition at Easter.'

'Extra runs at weekends,' said Rose, as they walked back

to the school after showering and changing. 'Count me out.'

'Don't you want to be on the team then?' asked Justice.

'Not really.' Rose shrugged but Justice suspected that she was lying. She thought that Rose would absolutely love to be on another school team.

'I think it sounds fun,' said Justice.

'Just because you've finally found a sport that you can do,' said Rose. 'And it's not very difficult, just running round a field.'

'If it's not difficult,' said Stella, 'why didn't you win?'

It was very unusual for Stella to sound so sharp. Rose and Alicia exchanged glances and Alicia said, obviously trying to change the subject, 'Who's auditioning for *Alice* at lunchtime?'

'I am,' said Justice. 'What about you, Stella?'

'I will if you will,' said Stella. 'I bet I won't get a part though. I think acting's awfully embarrassing.'

'You won't be Alice then,' said Rose. 'Nor will you, Justice. Your hair's too short.'

'I'd rather be the Queen of Hearts,' said Justice.

'Isn't she the awful one who keeps wanting to chop people's heads off? Yes, I can imagine that.'

'Off with her head,' muttered Justice as Rose strode ahead, blonde plaits gleaming in the winter sunlight.

*   *   *

Justice and Stella were the first to arrive for the auditions. Miss Crane, the English mistress, met them at the door of the assembly hall.

'Hallo. You're very prompt. Could you put some chairs out for me and Miss de Vere? I need to collect the scripts.' She hurried away, looking very much like the white rabbit.

The hall was empty but the stage curtains were pulled back, leaving an expectant-looking space.

'Oh, no,' said Stella. 'Do you think we've got to stand on the stage?'

'I suppose so,' said Justice. 'Where shall we put the chairs? In front of it?'

They put out two chairs and then Justice couldn't resist climbing on to the stage, just to see what it felt like. After a few minutes, Stella joined her.

'To be, or not to be . . .' Justice struck a Hamlet-like pose. Her voice echoed around the empty hall.

'Friends, Romans, countrymen . . .' Stella joined in.

When they'd used up their Shakespeare they started declaiming nursery rhymes. In the middle of 'Hickory, Dickory Dock', Justice grabbed Stella's arm.

'Listen!'

'What?'

'Someone's coming up the steps from the basement.'

When Justice and Stella had gone down to the basement last year, they had come up via a staircase that led into the assembly hall. This was reached by a small door at the side of the stage but, as far as Justice knew, it was usually kept locked. Now Justice and Stella drew back into the shadows and watched as the secret door opened slowly and Miss Robinson appeared. She looked around the room and made her way to the exit, walking very quickly. She was wearing gym shoes.

'What was Matron doing in the basement?' said Justice, as soon as the door closed. 'Miss de Vere said it was out of bounds.'

'That probably doesn't apply to teachers,' said Stella.

'Even so, what was she doing down there? There can't be any reason for her to go into the cellars.'

But, before Stella could answer, the doors opened and Miss Crane and Miss de Vere sailed in, followed by half a dozen aspiring actresses.

Justice thought that the audition went quite well. It was hard to tell. She really wanted a part in the play and that made her more nervous than usual. They had to read a speech by Alice, all about her falling down the rabbit hole and thinking that she might have ended up in Australia. Justice started off reading it too fast – she had to force herself to slow down and breathe properly. But at least she didn't stumble over the word 'Antipodes', as a lot of girls did, and Miss Crane even said 'Well done' afterwards. Justice thought about the play all afternoon until, in history, Miss Hunting said something that made her sit up.

'Highbury House is a Victorian building,' she was saying, 'but the cellars probably date back to Tudor times, when there was a manor house on this site.'

Justice put up her hand. 'Do you know a lot about the history of the house, Miss Hunting?'

Miss Hunting gave her a sharp look, as if she suspected her of cheek, but then she relented and said, 'As a matter of fact, I'm writing a book about the history of Highbury House. It's a fascinating subject.'

Behind Justice, Eva gave a soft groan. She obviously didn't think it was a fascinating subject. But Miss Hunting continued, 'In the reign of Queen Elizabeth, Catholics weren't allowed to say mass but some families continued in the old faith and they even had secret places in their houses where priests could hide. I think there's a priest hole *in this very school.*' She looked at the class impressively, the afternoon sun glinting on her silvery-blonde hair.

'A priest hole?' said Eva. 'You mean, like a rabbit hole?' *She's obviously still thinking about* Alice in Wonderland, thought Justice.

'Don't be stupid, Eva,' said Miss Hunting. 'I haven't yet found the priest hole, but I believe it's in the old part of the school.'

'In the basement?' said Justice.

'Possibly,' said Miss Hunting. 'Now, let's get back to the Wars of the Roses.'

Justice couldn't get much further with the Mystery of the Basement, but she thought about it all through that afternoon's lessons – Latin, maths and country dancing. Then, at meal, something happened to take her mind off detective work. A first year approached their table.

'Package for Justice Jones.'

It was a tuck box from Dad. The girls crowded round, oohing and aahing as Justice unpacked the contents: fruit cake, shortbread, chocolate biscuits, tins of pineapple chunks and fruit salad. The last item was a box of sweets with Grenadier Guards on the lid. Justice felt underneath. Yes, there it was. A note from Dad. Justice put it in her pocket to read later.

'Put that tuck away, Justice,' said Helena, from the

prefects' table. 'Only one item can be eaten at the table.'

Justice repacked the box and handed round the biscuits with a bland smile on her face. The Barnowls smiled back. They knew what a tuck box meant. It meant a midnight feast.

That night, as soon as Miss Robinson's heavy tread had died away, the Barnowls sat on the floor and began on the food. It was cold in the dormy but they wrapped themselves in blankets and Justice put her torch in the centre of the circle as if it was a camp fire. They passed round the pineapple chunks and fruit salad (Dad had helpfully included a tin opener and some spoons) and Justice cut the cake with her penknife. It reminded her of eating fruit cake at Smugglers' Lodge, with Sabre watching her.

Nora told ghost stories, holding the light under her chin to make her face look scary. After the one about The Thing That Walks At Night, Eva screamed. Rose told her not to be a rabbit and Eva promptly got hiccoughs. This started a giggling fit that soon spread to all the other girls. In other words, it was a typical midnight feast.

When she finally got into bed, Justice read Dad's letter by the light of her torch.

I hope term has started well and that you were pleased to see your friends again. If you find another mystery, try not to break too many school rules while solving it. And, most importantly, stay safe! I miss you greatly and look forward to seeing you on the February half holiday.

All love,

Dad

Justice put the note under her pillow and then settled down to sleep. But, a few minutes later, she sat up, switched her torch on again and wrote in her journal:

What was Miss Robinson doing in the basement? Could there be a secret priest hole there?

And how did Miss Morris know that Sabre was a guide dog?

CHAPTER 8

Justice was looking forward to her next visit to Smugglers' Lodge. It would be interesting to read the newspapers (at Highbury House the girls weren't even allowed to listen to the news on the wireless) and she would try to solve the mystery of Mr Arthur knowing about Dad, and Miss Morris knowing about Sabre. And maybe Mrs Kent would give her some more cake.

But, after breakfast on Wednesday, the day got even better.

Dorothy met her as the girls came out of the dining hall. She was carrying a tray of dirty plates and her eyes were shining.

'Guess what?'

'The new matron is a werewolf?'

'No, silly. My mum wrote to Miss de Vere asking if you could come to tea today. It's my half day and you'll be in the village anyway.'

'Did she say yes?' Justice could hardly believe it.

'She did! She said that you could come to our cottage for tea and that you and I could walk back to school together. It'll be safe in the dark with two of us.'

Justice gave a jump of joy. She'd always got the impression that the teachers disapproved of her friendship with Dorothy, yet here was the headmistress saying that she could go to Dorothy's house and meet her family. She couldn't wait.

The afternoon was bright and spring-like, the sun shining on the secret streams that zig-zagged across the marshes. Miss Heron set a brisk pace and, before long, the girls were taking off their gaberdines and hats. At the village green Miss Heron checked their names on her list and told them to be back at four-thirty. 'Except for Justice. I understand that you have permission to be out later.'

'Yes, Miss Heron.'

'Where are you going?' asked Rose. She was not in a good mood. On the last Good Citizenship afternoon, she'd had to help her family with the washing – which she said was 'maid's work'. She was threatening to write to her parents and complain.

'Secret assignment,' said Justice: Only Stella knew where she was going. She didn't want Rose making sneery remarks about Dorothy's family.

'I'll walk with you, Justice,' said Miss Heron. 'The rest of you, off you go.'

Why is Miss Heron accompanying me? thought Justice. She knew the way by now. But she didn't say anything and the two of them set off down the High Street.

The sea looked very different today – blue and sparkling, breaking against the stones in playful little waves. They stood on the shingle bank for a moment, looking at it. Then Miss Heron said, 'What sort of a man is Mr Arthur?'

'Well, he's blind,' said Justice.

'That's not who he *is*,' said Miss Heron rather fiercely. 'That's just something that happened to him.'

'I know,' said Justice. She felt rather ashamed of her first answer. 'He seems very nice,' she said. 'He told me that he was a pilot in the war and he still seems really keen on flying. He wants me to read the newspapers to him.'

'Is he interested in sport?' asked Miss Heron.

Justice suppressed a smile. The games mistress really was obsessed with her subject. She couldn't imagine anyone not being interested in it.

'I don't know,' she said. 'I didn't get to the sports pages last time.'

Miss Heron didn't seem to hear. She stooped, picked up a pebble and threw it into the sea. The stone skimmed over the water – once, twice, three times, glittering in the sun.

'Gosh, I wish I could do that,' said Justice.

'It's practice,' said Miss Heron. 'Like cross-country. Like everything. Have a good afternoon, Justice. Be careful walking home with Dorothy. Make sure you stick to the road.'

Justice knew that this was her cue to leave. She said goodbye and set off towards Smugglers' Lodge. But, when she looked back, Miss Heron was still staring at the sea.

This time Sabre didn't even bark. He looked up when Justice came into the room and wagged his tail as if to say, 'Welcome back. Now let's get on with the news.'

Mrs Kent made hot chocolate again, accompanied by deliciously spicy biscuits. Justice ate two but reluctantly decided that three would be greedy. She read aloud about floods and strikes and an airship called the *Hindenburg* that was being built in Germany. Mr Arthur was interested in this and asked her to read it again. Sabre's tail thumped on the floor.

When she'd finished reading, Mr Arthur looked towards the window as if he could see the view, the sky slowly darkening as twilight approached.

'How do you like the Romney Marshes, Justice?' he said.

'I like the sea,' said Justice. 'The marshes are a bit bleak. I'm only just getting to know the area really. We weren't allowed out of school last term.'

'I came here as a young man,' said Mr Arthur, still looking past her towards the window. 'And I loved it. The wide skies, the ever-changing sea. There was no sea where I was brought up.'

Justice wondered why he had come back, now that he could no longer see the sea and the sky. Mr Arthur smiled as if he understood. He stroked Sabre's ears.

'I came back because I'm looking for someone,' he said, as if she'd asked the question. 'Funny how I still use the words "look" and "see" even though I can't do either.'

'Who are you looking for?' asked Justice, aware that Miss Crane would say that the sentence was hopelessly ungrammatical.

'My daughter,' said Mr Arthur, still smiling.

'Your daughter?' Justice could hardly believe her ears.

'Yes. When I was here before the war, I married and had a daughter. Now I'm searching for her. That's another of those sight words, isn't it? But maybe you can search without being able to see.'

'Do you know where your daughter is?'

Mr Arthur didn't answer for a moment then, to Justice's surprise, he addressed the dog. 'Are we alone, Sabre?' Sabre gave a short bark. Then Mr Arthur looked at Justice and, for the first time, almost met her eyes. 'Can you keep a secret, Justice?'

'Yes!' said Justice. Slightly too eagerly, perhaps. She looked quickly around the room but, as Sabre had said, they were on their own.

'I think my daughter is at Highbury House Boarding School for the Daughters of Gentlefolk,' said Mr Arthur.

CHAPTER 9

Once again, Justice could hardly believe her ears. She stared at Mr Arthur, who was smiling vaguely in her direction. Sabre wagged his tail encouragingly.

'At my school?' she said at last.

'I think so,' said Mr Arthur. 'That's the last address I had for her, anyway. That's why I need you. I need you to be my detective.'

Justice's heart beat faster at these words. But, all the same, something wasn't quite right. *Why* did Mr Arthur need her?

'Why don't you just write to the headmistress?' she said. 'To Miss de Vere? She'd tell you.' She thought of the girls at her school, all two hundred odd of them. Which of them could be Mr Arthur's long-lost daughter?

'There are reasons why I can't approach Miss de Vere,' said Mr Arthur. 'And there are reasons why my daughter might not be happy to hear from me.'

'What reasons?' said Justice. She realised the question didn't sound very polite but, then again, she was meant to be a detective and detectives had to ask awkward questions.

'I can't tell you yet,' said Mr Arthur. 'Maybe when we know each other better. This is a house of secrets, Justice. The smugglers who once used this house had their own secrets. Let me keep mine for a while. In the meantime, will you help me?'

'Why me?' said Justice. 'I'm just a schoolgirl.'

'You're Herbert Jones's daughter,' said Mr Arthur, with a glimmer of a smile. 'And he's a brilliant lawyer and a fellow pilot. Also, I heard something about you solving a murder case at the school last year.'

'How did you hear that?' said Justice.

'Another secret, I'm afraid. But I know you are the one to help me. Why do you think I requested Herbert Jones's daughter as my Good Citizen?'

Justice gaped. Mr Arthur had requested her. This put a different slant on things. She was still speechless when Mrs Kent came into the room.

'It's nearly four-thirty, Justice. You'd better be on your way. Do you want to take the rest of the biscuits with you?'

Justice ran across the beach, slipping and sliding over the pebbles. It was almost dark now, but the sky seemed a tiny bit lighter than last week. Or was it just that she was feeling happier? At last she had a real mystery to solve, something more important than whether Miss Robinson was really a nurse. And she was going to meet Dorothy's family. She ran across the coast road and headed down the High Street, looking for Rectory Lane.

Dorothy's house was the last in a row of cottages, all built of flint with low roofs and different coloured front doors. Dorothy's was green and it opened before Justice had time to knock.

'I was waiting for you,' she said. 'You're five minutes late.'

'I ran all the way from Smugglers' Lodge,' said Justice.

'Dotty, let the poor girl get her breath back.' A woman appeared in the background. She was small with Dorothy's flyway hair and a welcoming smile.

'Hallo, Justice. I'm Hattie, Dorothy's mum. I must give you a hug. I feel like I know you so well.'

It was the first time that Dorothy had been hugged by a mum since her own had died. It wasn't the same; for one thing her mum had been quite tall and Hattie was only Justice's height, but it still felt wonderful. Just for a moment, Justice was scared that she might be about to cry.

Dorothy's mum patted her back as if she understood. 'Come in and sit down,' she said. 'I've got a good tea waiting. Dotty says it's horrible, the food they give you up at the school.'

'It is,' said Justice, feelingly.

The front door opened directly into a room which seemed crammed with furniture and people: a sofa, two chairs, a dresser and a round table with a checked cloth on it. Two girls were sitting on the sofa playing with dolls. Justice knew these must be Susan, aged ten, and Elsie, aged eight. Elsie was the one who had been ill and Justice thought that she still looked rather pale. A large baby sat on the floor, watching them.

Justice longed to join in with the girls' game, even though she had never been very keen on dolls. But she needed to get Dorothy on her own first. She wanted to tell her about Mr Arthur and his mysterious daughter.

But it was hard to be on your own in this wonderfully full house. 'We need to set the table for tea,' said Dorothy, in a capable, managing voice that Justice hadn't heard before.

'Johnny will be home soon,' said Susan. Justice knew

that John was twelve, her age, and the next oldest child after Dorothy. She asked where he was. 'He works on the farm in the evenings,' said Dorothy. 'Helping with the milking. He wants to be a farmer.'

Justice sat on the sofa with the younger girls. Elsie held up one of the dolls. 'This is Lady Penelope,' she said. 'Dotty makes up all sorts of stories about her.'

'I'm too old for dolls, really,' said Susan. 'I'm just keeping Elsie company because she hasn't been well.'

'How come you still sleep with your teddy bear, then?' retorted Elsie.

'So do I,' said Dorothy, 'and I'm fifteen. Now run along and wash your hands before tea.'

It felt strange seeing Dorothy be the elder sister. Justice was an only child, and she couldn't imagine what it would be like having siblings to look after – or order around. The younger girls got up immediately and went through the kitchen and out of the back door. Justice realised that the bathroom and toilet must be outside.

Dorothy picked up the baby and balanced him on her hip. 'This is Tommy,' she said. 'Isn't he big? Do you want to hold him?'

'No, thanks,' said Justice, backing away slightly. 'I might drop him.'

Dorothy looked slightly disappointed but, at that moment, the door opened and a man and a boy came in – Dorothy's father and brother. Dorothy's father, who was a cowman at the farm, was tall and ruddy-faced. He didn't talk much but, when he laughed, it was a loud 'Ho ho ho,' like someone playing Father Christmas. John was also tall, with dark hair and freckles. He was Justice's age, but seemed older.

'Dorothy's always talking about you,' he said.

'I'm not.' Dorothy blushed scarlet.

'Tea's ready,' said Hattie, coming in from the kitchen. 'Wash your hands, boys.'

Tea was the best meal Justice had eaten for ages, perhaps ever: ham, salad, boiled eggs, bread still warm from the oven, butter, cheese wrapped in a blue cloth. The children drank milk and the grown-ups had tea from a vast pot in a striped tea-cosy. The family talked about the farm, Susan's recent prize for reading and Tommy's new tooth. It was almost as noisy as the dining room at Highbury House, but much more cheerful. Justice thought of meals alone with her dad, where they both sometimes read all the way through – Dad looking through legal papers, Justice with a book propped up against her glass. It was companionable, but what would it be like to be part of a family like this, where everyone had their own news and opinions? Justice loved listening to them; the family's soft accents sounding so different from the clipped tones of the teachers at school. *Mr Arthur has a nice voice too*, she thought. It was unusual somehow.

'Justice was at Smugglers' Lodge today,' said Dorothy. She seemed determined to include her friend in the conversation.

'What were you doing there, Justice?' asked Hattie.

'Reading to Mr Arthur,' said Justice. 'It's part of some Good Citizen thing at school.'

'Mr Arthur seems a nice man,' said Hattie. 'Keeps himself to himself. I spoke to him once when he was walking with his guide dog on the beach. Beryl Kent's his housekeeper. I've heard that she keeps the place beautifully. It's a big old building.'

'Does Mr Arthur have any family?' asked Justice. She thought this might be a chance to find out about the mysterious daughter.

'I don't think so,' said Hattie. 'Mr Arthur said that, when he died, he was going to leave Smugglers' Lodge jointly to Mrs Kent and to his dog. He was joking, but it was rather sad, I thought.'

'Smugglers' Lodge is haunted,' said Susan. 'You can see the lights shining in the tower at night.'

'Why does it have a tower?' asked Justice. 'It seems strange.'

'It used to be the lighthouse,' said Hattie. 'The beach is treacherous, you see. Lots of sandbars where ships can run aground. And the coastline changes all the time. The lighthouse helped sailors come in to shore but it was hard to find people to work there and now the tower is empty, as far as I know. The house was empty too, until Mr Arthur came to live there.'

'Dorothy said that people used to shine lights to confuse the ships,' said Justice.

'A long time ago, that was,' said Hattie. 'The wreckers, they used to call them. They'd shine lanterns along the coast path, where the sandbars were. The ships would crash and the wreckers would steal everything on board. Wicked, I call it. Lots of the poor sailors drowned.'

'You can still hear them wailing, some nights,' said Susan.

'Rubbish,' said John. 'That's just the sea.'

'The Lodge was used for smuggling,' said Dorothy's dad, William, speaking for almost the first time. 'That's how it got its name. The village was famous for smuggling at one time. Even the vicar was in on it, they say. Some say that there are tunnels underneath the Lodge, going back into the village and even further, as far as Highbury House. The old lord, Lord Highbury, was said to be hand in glove with the smugglers.'

'Highbury House?' said Dorothy. 'But that's miles away.'

'It's not far, as the crow flies,' said her father. 'Less than a mile along the coast road.'

Justice thought of the house and of the tower with its strange lights. She thought of the way the wind had howled from the sea. She was glad that she was sitting in a warm room surrounded by people.

'Have some more cheese, Justice,' said Hattie. 'And there's treacle tart next.'

Justice wished that she could stay there for ever.

CHAPTER 10

It was nearly half-past seven by the time Justice and Dorothy left the cottage. They had to be back at school by eight but it was hard to leave, especially after the fire had been lit and Dorothy's parents listened to the wireless while the children played card games at the table. But Elsie had to go to bed at seven because she'd been ill and Susan had her homework to do. Justice and Dorothy put their coats on but then they were delayed because Hattie wanted to give them some cake and Elsie called down for them to say goodnight to her.

Elsie was sitting up in a double bed that almost filled the tiny room under the eaves. Where did Dorothy sleep when she was at home? wondered Justice. What about John?

There were only two bedrooms upstairs and she knew that the baby slept with his parents.

'Bye, Elsie,' said Justice. 'Sleep well.'

'Bye,' said Elsie. 'Come back and see us soon.'

'I will,' said Justice.

Dorothy kissed her sister and they descended the stairs. John met them in the hall.

'I'll walk you to the crossroads,' he said, holding up a lantern.

'We're not scared of the dark,' said Dorothy.

'And I've got a torch,' said Justice. But she was, secretly, quite pleased that John was accompanying them.

Hattie kissed Justice goodbye and told her to come again. William shook her hand and muttered something about being welcome any time. Dorothy kissed her parents and gave Susan a quick hug. Then they set off, John leading the way and Dorothy following with a cake tin under her arm.

As they crossed the village green, they saw that most of the houses were in darkness. The only light came from a fitful moon, scudding through the clouds.

'People go to bed early round here,' said Dorothy. 'They mostly work in the fields and have to be up at dawn.'

'Milking starts at five,' said John.

'Do you do that before school?' asked Justice. She found getting up at seven hard enough.

'Yes,' said John. 'But I can leave school next year.'

'Lucky you,' said Justice.

There was a single light glowing in the rectory. 'Probably the vicar thinking up a sermon,' said Justice. They passed the church and the graveyard, the tombstones looming at sinister angles. An owl hooted from the trees and Justice was glad of John's lantern and of her own trusty torch, showing the path that led to the marshes.

It wasn't long before they could see the signpost, white in the moonlight.

'People used to be buried at the crossroads,' said John. 'Murderers and vampires. Buried with wooden stakes through their hearts.'

'Don't,' said Dorothy.

'Vampires don't exist,' said Justice, but she moved a little closer to Dorothy.

The road across the marshes gleamed in front of them. In the village, the night had been clear, but here there were patches of mist appearing and disappearing like smoke.

'Will you be all right?' said John.

'Of course,' said Justice. 'It's not far from here. Bye, John.'

'Bye, Justice. Bye, Pie Face.'

Dorothy didn't deign to answer. She took Justice's hand and they set off along the empty road.

It seemed very dark after John and his lantern had left. The moon had disappeared and Justice's torch barely seemed to penetrate the blackness. But, for once, Justice hardly noticed her surroundings. She was desperate to tell Dorothy about Mr Arthur's search for his daughter.

'So she's a pupil at the school?' said Dorothy, as they trudged along, their footsteps echoing. 'Wouldn't it be funny if it was someone like Helena Bliss?'

Justice thought about Mr Arthur, sitting facing the view that he could no longer see. She heard him saying: *I was here before the war, I married and had a daughter*. She thought of Mr Arthur with his grey hair, looking so much older than her dad.

'Dorothy?' she said. 'Mr Arthur said that he was here before the war. That means before 1914. How old would you be now if you were born in 1914?' She knew that Dorothy was good at doing sums in her head.

'Twenty-five,' said Dorothy immediately. Then, realising what Justice meant, 'So Mr Arthur's daughter wouldn't be a pupil at the school. She's an adult.'

'That's right,' said Justice. 'She would be at least twenty-five, probably older. She would be . . .'

'A teacher,' Dorothy finished.

'Or someone else at the school.'

'Like Mrs Hopkirk.' Dorothy started to giggle. 'But she's about ninety. It can't be her.'

They were properly on the marshes now. There was darkness on either side, a sense of nothingness, as if they had strayed off the path into another world. Mist swirled in front of them. Even the night birds were silent.

'How far is it now?' said Dorothy.

'I don't know,' said Justice. 'The walk seemed to take no time at all this morning.'

'Shall we sing?' suggested Dorothy.

They sang 'One Man Went to Mow', 'This Old Man' and 'Amazing Grace'. They even tried the school song. But, after a while, their voices died away.

'We must be nearly at the turning now,' said Dorothy. 'Can you see the time?'

Justice shone her torch on her watch. 'Nearly eight.'

'Mrs Hopkirk will be furious if I'm late.'

'Do you think we've missed it?'

'I don't see how we could.'

Justice shone her torch. And there, in front of them, like a mirage, was the road to Highbury House. They were nearly there.

They hurried along, almost running. *It is strange*, thought Justice. In daylight you could see the school, with its turrets at each corner, from miles away. But now it was completely hidden by the fog, which was much thicker here. The gates appeared with terrifying suddenness, grey stone columns on either side.

'What if they're locked?' said Dorothy. But Justice pushed and the iron gate creaked open. Now they could see the school, a monstrous dark shape but with welcoming lights glowing on the ground floor. Justice went to shut the gate but, as she did so, she saw a movement in the bushes, a faint flicker of white.

Justice pulled Dorothy into the shade of the trees. 'Did you see that?' she whispered.

'What?'

'There's someone there. By the gates.'

As they watched, a figure emerged from the undergrowth and squeezed through the gap in the gates. A large woman wearing white gym shoes.

'Miss Robinson,' breathed Justice.

'What's she doing skulking in the grounds?' said Dorothy.

But the matron had vanished into the mist. Justice and Dorothy hurried across the lawn to the main entrance. The huge oak doors were bolted shut but there was a small door to one side that was still open. Once inside they took deep breaths.

'Well . . .' Dorothy began. But, before she could say more, Rose appeared, arm in arm with Alicia.

'Hallo, Justice. What are you doing coming in at this time? You've got mud on your shoes. Oh, and by the way, the cast list for *Alice* is up.'

Somehow Justice knew that it wasn't good news.

Alice: Helena Bliss. Well, Justice had expected that.

Queen of Hearts: Davina Sloane. Davina was another sixth former and Helena's best friend. Again, hardly a surprise.

White Rabbit: Rose Trevellian-Hayes. This was a blow. No wonder Rose had looked so smug.

Dormouse: Eva Harris.

Justice skimmed down the list of animals, playing cards and sundry made-up characters like Alice's parents and schoolfriends. Even Stella was there, as *Second Gardener*, but Justice's name was nowhere to be seen.

At last she found it. Right at the bottom. *Stage manager: Justice Jones*.

Stage manager! Not even a walk-on part! Justice's eyes stung with tears. She knew that Dorothy was looking at her sympathetically and somehow that made it worse.

'Sounds a stupid play anyway . . .' Dorothy began. But Justice turned away, wanting to run . . . where? That was the trouble with boarding school. There was nowhere that you could be on your own.

'Justice!' And there was another problem. Teachers. Justice turned and saw Miss de Vere gliding down the stairs towards her. 'Did you have a good time this afternoon?'

Justice had almost forgotten tea at Dorothy's house. To think that she'd been so happy, only an hour ago.

'Yes, thank you, Miss de Vere.'

Miss de Vere looked at her. Her expression was hard to read but it wasn't unsympathetic.

'Don't be too disappointed about the play,' she said. 'The stage manager is an important job. You see more from backstage.'

See more? But the headmistress swept away, leaving Justice to wonder exactly what she meant.

CHAPTER 11

'Stage manager is an important job. You'll be responsible for all the props and for making sure that everyone is where they should be. You'll be in charge, really.'

Justice sighed. Mr Arthur was trying to be kind but, as far as Rose and the others were concerned, she was the lowest of the low. She'd tried to be nice about it and to congratulate her friends on their roles. But Stella had known that she was upset. She'd even offered to swap with her. 'I don't want to be the second gardener, whoever that is.' That just made it worse. Stella didn't even want to be in the play and she had a part. Justice had wanted desperately to be in *Alice*, she'd done a reasonable audition, she had a good memory for lines and was one of the best at reading aloud in class. Why hadn't she been chosen?

But she tried to make her voice sound cheerful when she answered Mr Arthur. 'It doesn't matter,' she said. 'It's only a school play.' That was what Dad had said, when she'd told him the news in her weekly letter. He was right, of course, but Dad didn't understand that, at boarding school, little things took on epic proportions. The play was all anyone could talk about. Helena Bliss had taken to wearing a headband like Alice and Rose was making herself a pair of fluffy ears to play the White Rabbit.

'And you were picked for the cross-country team,' said Mr Arthur. 'One of only four in the year.'

Justice no longer read from *The Times*, unless there was something in it about flying. Now Justice and Mr Arthur just chatted for their two hours together. He seemed endlessly fascinated by school life.

'Rose is in the cross-country team too,' said Justice.

'You mustn't measure everything by Rose,' said Mr Arthur sternly. 'You can't let her play such a big role in your life.' Justice thought that she could see Sabre nodding in the background.

'I used to be a runner once,' Mr Arthur continued. 'I loved the sense of freedom.'

'There's not much freedom when you're running round the school fields,' said Justice, but she knew what he meant. The team had been out for a couple of evening runs with Miss Heron. These had been more serious affairs than the weekly cross-country practice but Justice had enjoyed pounding along the roads at dusk, mesmerised by the sound of her footsteps, pushing deeper and deeper to produce better and better finish times.

'Let's talk about Operation Daughter,' she said, producing her notebook. 'Tell me again how much you remember.'

'Are you writing this down?' said Mr Arthur, smiling. 'I last saw Bunny when she was fourteen. She was such a pretty girl, full of life. I left in 1914 to go to war. When I was away, Bunny's mother divorced me and told me not to contact her again. Last year I heard that my ex-wife had died, so I decided to come back to Romney Marsh. I had heard that Bunny was at the school and I wrote to her but I got no reply.' He paused. 'That's why I decided to employ a private detective.'

He must mean her. Justice couldn't help feeling proud. She wasn't in *Alice* but she was a private detective. 'What was Bunny's real name again?' she said.

'Hildegarde. But she never used it.'

I'm not surprised, thought Justice. 'Hildegarde what?'

'My ex-wife went back to her maiden name, which was Williams.'

'There's no Miss Williams at the school,' said Justice. They had been through this many times before. 'What colour was her hair?'

'Blonde. And she had blue eyes.'

Justice couldn't think of a blonde teacher, except . . . An image came to her of Miss Heron running along beside her, yellow ponytail flying.

'How old would Bunny be now?' she said.

'Thirty-seven.'

Could Miss Heron be thirty-seven? She seemed quite young compared to the other teachers. Justice would have to do some sleuthing.

'Time to go, Justice.' Mrs Kent appeared in the doorway. 'I've got some rock cakes for you.'

'Thank you,' said Justice. Coming to Smugglers' Lodge was almost like getting a tuck box every week.

'Goodbye,' she said to Mr Arthur. 'See you next Wednesday.'

'Goodbye, Justice,' said Mr Arthur, smiling in her direction. 'Remember, you are a detective and detectives never give up.' Sabre wagged his tail in agreement.

*   *   *

In fact, Justice didn't see Mr Arthur the next week because it was the half holiday. Dad came down and they drove to Jury's Gap, a beach a few miles away, and had lunch in the pub. Justice had invited Stella to join them but, at the last minute, her father got the family car mended and all the Goldmans made the trip. Justice was happy for her friend and even happier to have Dad to herself.

It was a beautiful early spring day. They walked on the beach and collected shells. Justice remembered her dad telling her that there had been lots of shipwrecks on this part of the coast. She thought of Smugglers' Lodge and of the false lights luring the sailors on to the rocks.

'Did you look for Mr Arthur in the RFC files?' she asked Dad, as they turned towards the pub. In one of her letters Justice had asked him to find Mr Arthur in the Royal Flying Corps records. She had some idea that Mr Arthur might like a memento of his time as an airman. He still enjoyed stories about flying, especially the *Hindenburg* airship.

'Yes,' said Dad. He seemed to be making up his mind whether to say more, but then he continued, 'I'm sorry, Justice, but your Mr Arthur isn't listed in any of the archives.'

'He must be!'

'I've checked very thoroughly.'

'How can that be possible?'

'Well . . .' Dad paused. 'Either his records have got lost or Mr Arthur was never in the RFC.'

'He was. He told me that he was a pilot.' He had talked about Dad as a 'fellow pilot' too.

Dad said nothing until they were seated at the table with their food in front of them. Then he said, 'What sort of a man is Mr Arthur?'

'He's nice,' said Justice. 'He really listens when you talk. I've told him all about cross-country and . . . about the play.'

'You're not still disappointed about that, are you?'

'No. Yes. A bit. It helps having something else to think about. I'm helping Mr Arthur find his long-lost daughter.'

Dad put his knife and fork down. 'I beg your pardon?'

Justice told him about Mr Arthur's search for his daughter. She hadn't wanted to put this in a letter because the old matron used to read all their letters and presumably Miss Robinson did the same. Dad seemed very interested.

'It's not Miss de Vere,' he said. 'I met her father once. He's a vicar. Lives on the Isle of Wight.'

'The daughter's quite old,' said Justice. 'Thirty-seven.'

'That's not old,' said Dad, laughing. 'I'm forty-four.'

'You're different,' said Justice.

'That's just because I'm your dad,' said Herbert. 'I'll still think of you as my little girl, even when you're thirty-seven.'

'I can't imagine being that old,' said Justice.

Herbert smiled. 'I wonder what you'll be doing when you're thirty-seven? Perhaps you'll be a lawyer like me.'

Justice didn't want to be a lawyer – she was going to be a detective, but she didn't want to hurt Dad's feelings. Besides, it was impossible to think of herself at that age. Maybe she'd even be married with children by then? But that seemed an even more impossible thought. Her dream was to be like Leslie Light in Mum's books, who taught at a university and solved crimes in his spare time. You never saw Leslie doing any actual teaching (his students never appeared unless they were suspects) and you certainly never learnt anything about his private life, if he had one.

'I can't think that far ahead,' she said. 'Even the end of term seems years away.'

Dad laughed and they talked about something else. All too soon, it was time to drive back to Highbury House. The sun was setting over the sea as they crossed the marshes, making the shadow of their car seem impossibly tall. The long grass was undulating like water, strangely light against the darkening sky.

'It's a beautiful landscape in its own way,' said Dad.

'I'll take your word for it,' said Justice.

She thought of walking back in the dark with Dorothy, the way the fog seemed to swallow up every landmark. Justice was glad of the sturdy Lagonda (Bessie was their name for it) and of Dad's strong, capable hands on the wheel. By the time they reached the school it was almost completely dark and the towers and battlements were doing their usual impression of Dracula's castle.

To Justice's surprise, Miss de Vere was waiting for them at the main entrance.

'Did you have a good day out?' she asked Justice.

'Yes, thank you, Miss de Vere.'

'How's the law treating you?' she asked Justice's dad. Something about her tone made Justice feel uneasy. She knew that her father and her headmistress were acquainted but Miss de Vere's voice sounded friendly, almost *playful*. It was embarrassing to listen to.

'I can't complain,' said Dad. 'How's the life of a headmistress?'

'I probably could complain,' said Miss de Vere, 'but I won't. I wonder if I could have a word, after you've said goodbye to Justice?'

'Of course,' said Herbert, but Justice thought that he sounded a little wary.

'I'll be in my study,' said Miss de Vere. 'Justice will tell you the way.'

Then, to Justice's relief, Miss de Vere drifted away, leaving her to say goodbye to Dad. He hugged her and whispered, 'Love you. See you soon.'

'Love you too.' Justice hugged him tightly. She felt tears rising up but she fought them down fiercely. She would see Dad at Easter and, in the meantime, she had things to do:

1. Solve the mystery of Mr Arthur's daughter, Bunny.
2. Discover why Miss Robinson is always sneaking around at night.
3. Find out why Miss de Vere needed to talk to Dad in private.

After all, Herbert Jones QC was Justice's father, but he was also a lawyer. And why would someone want to see a lawyer unless they'd committed a crime?

CHAPTER 12

Justice couldn't find a way of questioning Miss de Vere but, two days after the half holiday, she received a letter from Dad with an intriguing PS: 'Watch out for the new matron, Miss Robinson. I think that there might be some mystery about her.' *Watch out for the new matron.* There it was in black and white. There *was* some mystery about Miss Robinson. Was this why Miss de Vere had wanted to see Dad?

Justice was worried. The old matron used to read their letters to their parents and their parents' letters back. If Miss Robinson did the same, she would know that Dad suspected her of something. But, whereas last term their letters had clearly been opened before they received them, this term there was no sign that they had been tampered with.

'Does Matron still read our letters from home?' Justice asked Stella. The post always arrived when they were at breakfast and was delivered to the tables by a first year. This morning it was a very bumptious girl called Sally, who handed over each letter with a mocking bow. Justice put hers in her blazer pocket.

'I don't think so,' said Stella. 'I told my mother about Miss Loomis's wart and nothing happened to me.'

'A wart's not the same as being a criminal,' said Justice. She told Stella about Dad's PS.

'He doesn't say that she's a criminal,' said Stella. 'He says there's some mystery.'

'What else can it be?' said Justice. 'My father's a criminal lawyer. This must be why Miss de Vere wanted to see him after the half holiday.'

'Maybe it's to do with the other thing,' said Stella. 'Operation Daughter.' Justice had told her friend all about Mr Arthur's search for Bunny.

'If that was it, he'd say,' said Justice. 'I told Dad about Operation Daughter. This must be something else. Something more sinister.'

'What are you doing standing around chatting, girls?' It was Helena Bliss, wafting over from the prefects' table. 'You should be getting to lessons.'

'Yes, Helena,' said Stella.

'Curiouser and curiouser,' said Justice.

'What's that, Justice?' said Helena, fixing her with an icy blue stare.

'I was quoting from *Alice in Wonderland*,' said Justice, trying to look innocent. 'Well, I'm sure you know that, because you're Alice in the play.'

This was rather daring because Helena had, in fact, been rather slow to learn Alice's lines. Everyone else was word perfect by now, but Justice often had to prompt Helena.

'Don't be cheeky, Justice,' said Helena. 'Just because you're the stage manager. Hurry up and get to class now.'

'Oh dear, oh dear,' said Justice, 'I shall be too late.' She was quoting the White Rabbit but she didn't think that Helena noticed. Monsieur Pierre was walking by, carrying a tottering pile of grammar books. Helena rushed to help him. She was well known to have a crush on the French master.

It wasn't so bad, really, being the stage manager. Miss Crane was meant to be the producer but she didn't always come to the rehearsals, which meant that Justice was in charge. It was quite fun telling Helena Bliss where to stand and what to do (not that she took any notice). Justice also enjoyed finding props and costumes. It was an excuse to escape sometimes. Last Sunday, when it was raining outside and Justice had been missing Dad and not wanting to talk to anyone, she had spent a cosy afternoon in the art room making giant playing cards. After a few hours, Stella had joined her and they had worked together companionably, not talking much but taking comfort from each other's presence.

There was a rehearsal at lunchtime that day involving Helena and a girl called Chona, who was playing the caterpillar. Justice arrived early to set up the props. In the book, the caterpillar sits on a toadstool. One was being specially made for the performance, but today Chona would have to sit on a table. Justice was on stage arranging the set when she heard a sound coming from outside. She thought it might be the actors arriving and peeped out from behind the curtains. But instead of Helena swanning in wearing her Alice band, she saw the basement door opening and Miss Robinson emerging.

As she had done before, the matron looked round the room and then walked quickly towards the exit. But she had left the door to the basement open. Did Justice dare go down there? Miss de Vere had said that it was strictly out of bounds. But why? Why make such a point of telling the girls not to go into the cellars? Most of them would never dream of it anyway. It must be because she had something to hide. That's what Lesley Light would say, anyway. She remembered Dad's PS. *Watch out for the new matron, Miss Robinson. I think that there might be some mystery about her.*

Justice climbed down from the stage. She took one look around the hall but there was no sign of Helena and Chona. Justice went to the door at the side of the stage. Almost before she knew what she was doing, Justice started to descend the stairs. At the bottom there was a stone corridor with a low, curved ceiling. Justice remembered this from her previous visit. She edged along the brick wall, wishing she had her torch. Then she heard a most unwelcome sound. Footsteps approaching, moving very fast, echoing in the enclosed space. Justice looked around wildly. There was an alcove nearby with barrels in it. Justice squeezed herself in and crouched down behind the barrels. The footsteps got closer and closer and Justice saw a figure emerging. Tweed skirt, green jumper, greyish hair. In the dim light it could be any of the teachers but, as the figure came closer, Justice saw that it was Miss Hunting, the history teacher. Luckily, Miss Hunting did not look right or left. She walked quickly towards the stairs and Justice heard her footsteps ascending and then the door at the top clicking shut. *Don't let it be locked*.

Justice waited a few minutes, then she crept out and sprinted along the corridor. There was a piece of paper at the bottom of the staircase. A clue! Justice picked it up and put it in her pocket. Then she climbed the steps and pushed at the door. Thank goodness it wasn't locked. Justice emerged into the hall, which was quite deserted. She brushed herself down – she seemed to be covered in dust – and headed to the stage. As she did so, the main doors opened and Helena Bliss stalked in.

'Buck up, Justice,' she said. 'I thought you'd be prepared for this rehearsal. I haven't got all day, you know.'

Justice didn't get a chance to look at the clue until the rehearsal was over. Then she ran quickly upstairs to the second form common room. It was empty because everyone was queuing for lunch. It was a mystery to Justice why everyone was always so keen to see what was for lunch – whatever it was it was sure to be horrible – but today she was glad of it. Justice sat on the sofa and smoothed out the piece of paper and began to read.

Dear Bunny,
    I know you will be surprised to hear from me.
But I hope it won't be an altogether unwelcome
one. I am your father, my dear, and I am living
nearby, in a house called Smugglers' Lodge.
I would so love to see you again. I know that
you might think of me as an enemy but

Here the writer reached the end of the page. Justice turned it over. There was nothing on the back. There was presumably a page two and probably a page three. Was the letter from Mr Arthur? It must be, surely? If so, was Miss Hunting Bunny? Was Miss Robinson? The paper may well have been dropped before Justice entered the basement. She might just have missed it the first time she passed.

'Justice! What are you doing in here?'

It was Miss Morris, glaring from behind her little gold-rimmed spectacles.

Justice scrunched the letter up in her hand. 'I was looking for my maths book,' she said. She didn't know why she said this, perhaps because Miss Morris also taught maths.

'Indeed?' Miss Morris looked around the room, which

was full of half-finished jigsaws and pieces of embroidery. There were a few books too, face down on the table and on the chairs. 'You should take better care of your possessions.'

'Yes, Miss Morris.'

'Go downstairs for lunch,' said Miss Morris. 'You need to eat well at your age.'

Eating well would mean skipping most of Cook's meals, thought Justice. But she got up.

'Yes, Miss Morris.' She slipped the paper into her pocket. She tried to be subtle about it but she was pretty sure that her form mistress had seen.

She didn't get a chance to tell Stella until they were getting ready for bed.

'Could Miss Hunting be the daughter?' said Stella, as they pulled the curtains at the end of the dormy.

'I wouldn't have thought so,' said Justice. 'Isn't she too old? She's got grey hair.'

'It is a sort of greyish blonde,' said Stella. 'Miss Heron's the only teacher with properly blonde hair.'

'It looks like Miss Heron's our best bet,' said Justice. 'I would have thought that she's younger than thirty-seven though.'

'Maybe all that exercise has kept her young,' said Stella.

'Maybe. Her name's not Hildegarde though. I looked at the label on her tennis racket press and it said, "Margaret Heron".'

'She's probably changed it. I would.'

'Me too,' said Justice. 'But what about the letter? It looks as if someone dropped it down in the basement. That could only be Miss Hunting or Miss Robinson. Matron.'

'Surely Matron's too old,' said Stella. 'And not blonde.'

'I can't imagine her being called Bunny, either,' said Justice. They both started to laugh.

'Hurry up and pull those curtains, Stella and Justice,' called Rose from the other end of the room. 'There's a horrible draught coming through.'

Rose was right. The wind was getting up. Justice could see the tops of the trees blowing crazily. The moon was shining behind the tower, illuminating the windows where, it was said, you could sometimes see Grace Highbury's white face looking out. Justice pulled the curtains and went to get her washing kit.

When she was in bed, Justice got out her journal. She wrote:

OPERATION DAUGHTER
Who is Bunny?
1. Miss Heron.
   Pro: blonde hair, seemed interested in Mr Arthur.

> _Anti_: too young?
> 2. Miss Hunting.
>   _Pro_: may have dropped letter in the basement.
>   _Anti_: too old, has never shown any interest in Mr Arthur.
> 8. Miss Robinson.
>   _Pro_: was in the basement today, keeps popping up in odd places, may not be a proper nurse. Dad says there's some mystery about her.
>   _Anti_: dark hair. Too old?
> 4. All the other teachers: too old, no one blonde (though, as Stella put it, some are greyish blonde), no one interesting enough (except Miss de Vere and it's not her).
> _NB_: Must solve mystery of the cellars and the basement.

Justice closed her journal and slipped it under the loose floorboard. Then she closed her eyes and tried to sleep. But the windows were rattling and she could hear the wind howling across the marshes. Normally, she would quite enjoy being warm inside while a storm raged outside, but tonight she felt curiously unsettled, as if something bad was going to happen.

The next morning Miss de Vere told her that Mr Arthur had died in the night.

CHAPTER 13

'I'm sorry,' said Miss de Vere. 'The housekeeper said you were fond of him.'

Justice was in Miss de Vere's study in the South Turret. She'd been summoned there after breakfast and her first, terrified, thought was that something had happened to Dad. Afterwards she was ashamed that, when she first heard about Mr Arthur, her immediate reaction was relief that Dad was safe. Afterwards, though, other feelings came rushing in.

'He was nice to me,' she said. 'I enjoyed talking to him.' She thought of the afternoons at Smugglers' Lodge, drinking hot chocolate and eating homemade cake, chatting to Mr

Arthur while Sabre looked on. Tears came to her eyes and she fumbled for a handkerchief.

'What's going to happen to Sabre, Mr Arthur's dog?' she asked.

'I'm afraid I don't know,' said Miss de Vere. 'It was the housekeeper, Mrs Kent, who informed me this morning. She thought you'd want to know.'

'Thank you,' said Justice. *It was kind of Mrs Kent*, she thought. It seemed awful to think that, otherwise, she wouldn't have known until she turned up at Smugglers' Lodge on Wednesday. She wondered what had happened. Mr Arthur hadn't seemed ill when Justice last saw him. He was blind, but people didn't suddenly die of blindness, did they?

'Miss de Vere?' she said. 'How did Mr Arthur die?'

The headmistress looked at her as if she was wondering how much to say. 'I'm telling you this because I know I can trust you to be sensible, Justice,' she said. 'Also, because it will be common knowledge in a few days.' Justice pricked up her ears and leant forward.

Miss de Vere smiled slightly. 'Don't look so excited, Justice. It's nothing for you to get involved with. Just a tragic incident, a robbery gone wrong. Mr Arthur was shot.'

'Shot?' Justice could hardly believe that the headmistress had said the word.

'Mrs Kent found Mr Arthur in his armchair by the window. It looks as if intruders broke in and shot him. A window was broken and there were signs of forced entry.'

'He was shot by a burglar?' echoed Justice. Something was wrong here. 'What about Sabre? He wouldn't let anyone hurt Mr Arthur.'

'It seems as if someone fed the dog poisoned meat. He has recovered now, I think.'

'Someone poisoned Sabre and killed Mr Arthur? Why? Was anything stolen?'

'I don't know the answers to your questions, Justice,' said Miss de Vere, 'but I'm sure the police are investigating. All that we can do is mourn poor Mr Arthur. I will excuse you from the first lesson this morning. Go for a walk in the grounds or read a book in the library.'

'Thank you,' said Justice automatically. At boarding school, you were expected to thank the teachers for everything, even giving you detention. 'Miss de Vere? Do you think I might be able to go to Mr Arthur's funeral? I'd like to . . . pay my respects.'

She was pleased with this phrase, which she thought sounded grown-up and serious. And she did want to say goodbye to Mr Arthur. In a few weeks, he'd become a friend. But she also wanted to solve the mystery of his death.

Because she was sure that there was one.

'I'll see,' said Miss de Vere, giving her one of her searching looks. 'You might find it too upsetting.'

Because of Mum, Justice thought. People didn't realise that, if your mother dies, it's so terrible that nothing else even comes close. Everything reminded her of Mum, not just funerals and people dying. But she didn't say this aloud. She had learnt to keep these feelings secret.

'I think he would have liked me to go,' said Justice. 'I don't think he knew many people round here.' She remembered Dorothy's mother saying that Mr Arthur 'kept himself to himself'.

'Maybe,' said Miss de Vere. 'I'll talk to Mrs Kent. You might be able to attend. With a teacher, of course.'

Like a prisoner being allowed out for a day, thought Justice.

'Thank you, Miss de Vere,' she said.

Justice walked slowly down the spiral staircase that led to the first-floor corridor. She still couldn't believe that Mr Arthur was dead, that she'd never see him again. That was what she remembered about the awful days after her mother had died. It was that realisation, happening again and again, morning after morning, that her mum was actually gone, that she'd never talk to her or hug her again. But she didn't want to think about Mum. Instead she would think about the mystery. Because this was another mystery, no doubt about it. And this was the most serious investigation of all because someone had been killed, someone Justice knew and liked. And, when she came to think about it, there were a lot of unanswered questions. Why would a burglar break into Smugglers' Lodge, shoot Mr Arthur and poison his dog? It didn't make sense. Mr Arthur was blind, he couldn't hurt an intruder. There was no reason to kill him, except for the fact that someone clearly wanted him dead. Why?

'Justice. What are you doing out of lessons?'

It was Miss Heron, wearing her running clothes – divided skirt and cricket jumper.

'Miss de Vere said I could miss the first lesson,' said Justice. 'She's just told me about Mr Arthur.'

She wondered if the teachers knew, but a glance at Miss Heron's face told her that they did. The games mistress looked positively red-eyed. Why did she look so sad about a man she'd never met? Unless she really was his daughter, of course. Justice remembered Miss Heron questioning her after her first visit to the house on the edge of the beach. *What sort of a man is Mr Arthur?*

'I'm sorry,' said Miss Heron. 'I know you enjoyed your afternoons at Smugglers' Lodge.'

'Yes,' said Justice. 'I did. He was a nice man.' It felt wrong to use the past tense. She remembered that about Mum too.

Miss Heron took out a handkerchief and blew her nose. Then she said, 'I tell you what, Justice. Let's go for a run. There's nothing like running for taking your mind off things.'

'I've got to be back for next lesson,' said Justice. 'It's history.'

'We'll just go round the top field,' said Miss Heron. 'Go and get your running shoes.'

It was strange, running with Miss Heron, almost as if they were friends rather than teacher and pupil. They skirted the field, the mist still clinging to the valley, the birds singing high up in the pale blue sky. Justice tried to match her pace to Miss Heron but, as they started up the last slope, the teacher drew ahead. It was if she was sprinting the last hundred yards.

They met by the gymnasium – Justice panting, Miss Heron hardly out of breath.

'You're such a fast runner,' said Justice.

'Practice,' said Miss Heron. 'That's all it is.'

'Ninety per cent perspiration,' said Justice, mopping her brow with her sleeve. 'Like Miss de Vere said in her assembly.'

To her surprise, Miss Heron laughed. 'Yes,' she said. 'Glad you were playing attention.'

They walked back to the school, Miss Heron striding ahead. Three wild rabbits were playing on the front lawn.

'Bunny!' said Justice loudly.

But Miss Heron didn't even look round.

Justice found it hard to concentrate in history, even though it was usually her favourite subject. She kept thinking about Mr Arthur, shot dead in his chair. Who would have wanted to kill such a sweet and gentle man? She stared at Miss Hunting, as she tried to explain the origins of the Wars of the Roses. Could the history teacher possibly be Mr Arthur's missing daughter? She tried to think about everything that she knew about Miss Hunting. She was a good teacher, but inclined to be strict and sharp-tongued. Justice didn't mind this so much because she was usually concentrating in history lessons. Like all the teachers, Miss Hunting had never told them anything about her private life, aside from the fact that she had once owned a dog called

Prinny, after the Prince Regent. Mr Arthur had liked dogs too. Could this be a sign that they were related?

'Justice!' Miss Hunting's voice cut through her thoughts. 'Could you summarise what I've just told you about Warwick the King Maker?'

Justice thought wildly. 'He was from Warwick and he . . . er . . . made kings.' How did he do it again? Did he have some kind of workshop? 'Some people thought Warwick was cruel,' she invented, 'but other people thought he was as gentle as . . . as a bunny.'

Somebody laughed and turned it into a cough. Miss Hunting stared at her coldly. 'You may take an order mark for not paying attention, Justice. Kindly read through the chapter on Warwick and hand me a precis in the morning.'

Miss Hunting hadn't reacted to the word 'bunny', thought Justice, beyond looking annoyed. And, if she was Mr Arthur's daughter, she didn't seem heart-broken that her father had just died. But maybe she hated her father? Justice remembered the unfinished line in the letter: *I know that you might think of me as an enemy* . . . She saw Miss Hunting staring at her and hastily looked down at her book.

*   *   *

118

In prep, Justice started reading the chapter on Warwick, which was actually quite interesting. Then a sentence caught her attention, 'In addition to this, Warwick owned three islands off the coast of Britain: Jersey, Guernsey and Alderney . . .' Islands, island . . . What did that remind her of? Oh yes, Miss de Vere's assembly on the first day of term. Justice shut the book and went to the shelf where the big reference volumes were kept. She searched in the *Oxford Dictionary of Quotations* until she found the poem that Miss de Vere had quoted.

No man is an island entire of itself; every man
is a piece of the continent, a part of the main;
if a clod be washed away by the sea, Europe
is the less, as well as if a promontory were, as
well as any manor of thy friends or of thine
own were; any man's death diminishes me,
because I am involved in mankind.
And therefore never send to know for whom
the bell tolls; it tolls for thee.

Mr Arthur's death diminished all of them. She had to find out what had happened to him. She copied out the poem in her journal and, underneath, she wrote:

THE DEATH OF MR ARTHUR.

'Assemble the facts and look for a pattern.'

That was a quote from the Leslie Light books.

Suspicious factors:

1. Why kill him? Mr A could not have fought an intruder.
2. Mr A was killed sitting in his chair so he couldn't have known about the 'intruder'. Why not? A breaking window would make a noise and Mr A's hearing was very good.
3. Sabre was poisoned. That means that someone a) knew that Mr A had a dog and b) what he liked to eat. (Oh, I do hope Sabre is all right!)
4. Mr A was shot. What sort of small-town burglar has a gun?

Conclusion: Mr Arthur wasn't killed by burglars.

Someone murdered him.

WHY?

CHAPTER 14

Justice didn't know if Miss de Vere had spoken to Mrs Kent or whether she had just had a change of heart, but the headmistress decided that Justice could attend the funeral, which was held in the village church on the following Wednesday. Miss Morris drove Justice there in her car which would, in normal circumstances, have been a great treat. The village was quiet and many of the cottages had their curtains closed as a sign of respect but the church bell was ringing when they approached and, once again, Justice thought of the poem. *And therefore never send to know for whom the bell tolls; it tolls for thee.*

Justice was surprised to see Miss Heron waiting by the gate.

The games mistress was wearing a black coat and hat which made her look older than normal and more like a teacher.

'Hallo, Margaret,' said Miss Morris. Then, with a quick glance at Justice, 'Miss Heron, I mean. I would have given you a lift if I'd known.'

'That's all right,' said Miss Heron. 'I like walking, as you know.'

They entered the church and Justice heard Miss Morris give an exclamation of surprise. There, sitting in the shadows at the back, was Miss Robinson, looking scarier than ever in deepest black.

'Did you know Matron was coming?' Miss Morris muttered to Miss Heron.

'No, I didn't. It seems . . .' But Miss Heron did not complete the sentence and neither teacher approached the school matron. Miss Morris led them to one of the middle pews and they sat down.

Justice didn't remember much about her mother's funeral. It was as if the whole day had vanished in an awful blur. But she had a dim recollection of the church being full of people and flowers. Today, apart from Mrs Kent and a few others right at the front, there were only Justice, Miss Morris, Miss Heron and, at the back, Miss Robinson. *It is sad*, thought Justice, *that Mr Arthur's housekeeper is in the pew where his family should be*. But, then again, maybe he didn't have any close family. Apart from his missing daughter, who might well be sitting right next to Justice.

Mr Arthur's coffin was brought in by the undertaker's men. There was something very sad about the shiny oak casket. There were no flowers apart from a single bouquet of red and white roses on top of the coffin. Justice would have given a lot to know who it was from.

The service was very quick. Just two hymns, one reading and a brief sermon from the vicar, saying how bravely Frederick had borne his misfortunes. It took Justice a few minutes to realise that Frederick was Mr Arthur's first name. Well, Frederick Arthur had certainly had his misfortunes; he had lost his sight in the war, his wife divorced him and he lost contact with his only child. But Justice remembered a kind, gentle man who laughed at funny news items in the papers or at Justice's description of the food at Highbury House. Misfortune hadn't made him bitter or angry. Mr Arthur had been genuinely interested in the world and in the schoolgirl who came to visit. Justice felt her eyes prickling again. She noticed Miss Heron dabbing her eyes. Miss Morris stared straight ahead.

Then, after one more hymn, the voices sounding very thin in the near-empty church, the coffin was carried out for what the vicar called a 'private interment'. Miss Morris gathered up her bag and gloves and indicated that they should leave. As Justice was walking down the aisle, she saw that Mrs Kent was waiting for her.

The housekeeper was also dressed in black and her face looked pale and strained but she smiled when she saw Justice.

'It was so good of you to come.'

'I wanted to,' said Justice, feeling awkward. 'I liked Mr Arthur.'

'He liked you too.' Mrs Kent turned to Miss Morris. 'I was wondering if Justice could come back to the house to choose a keepsake of Mr Arthur's. I'm sure that's what he would have wanted.'

Miss Morris hesitated for a moment and then said, 'Very well, but we can't stay very long. We have to be back at the school for lunch.'

That's right, thought Justice, *wouldn't want to miss one of Cook's delicious feasts*. She hoped that Mrs Kent might have baked some cakes. When Mum died all the neighbours seemed to give them cakes, not that Justice had felt up to eating at the time.

'Mrs Kent?' she said. 'Is Sabre all right?'

Mrs Kent smiled. 'He's fine. Perkins, Mr Arthur's chauffeur, is looking after him.' She turned to Miss Morris.

'Sabre was Mr Arthur's guide dog. An Alsatian. A lovely animal.'

'German Shepherds are very intelligent dogs,' said Miss Morris.

'Oh, yes,' said Mrs Kent. 'I could swear Sabre understands every word I say. I almost expect him to answer me sometimes.'

Justice wished Sabre could speak, then he could tell her who murdered his master. But she didn't see any point in saying this aloud. Miss Morris said that she would give Mrs Kent a lift and they walked through the churchyard to the car. Miss Heron and Miss Robinson seemed to have vanished.

Miss Morris parked not far from Smugglers' Lodge. Together they crossed the shingle beach and climbed the steps to the front door. The house seemed very empty without Mr Arthur and Sabre. Justice saw Mr Arthur's chair in its usual place by the window.

'Where did the burglars get in?' she asked. Miss Morris frowned at her but Mrs Kent answered, 'Through the kitchen. I always leave a window slightly open at the top and they must have thrown in the poisoned meat, waited for Sabre to eat it and then broken the glass.'

'Why didn't Mr Arthur hear the glass breaking?'

'It was a windy night,' said Mrs Kent. 'I sleep directly upstairs and I didn't hear anything above the noise of the storm.'

That was a possible explanation, Justice conceded.

'Did Mr Arthur usually sleep in his chair?' she asked.

Mrs Kent gave her a slightly quelling look but she answered, 'No. His bedroom was on the ground floor, but Mr Arthur often sat in his chair until late in the evening.'

'Did the burglars steal anything?' asked Justice.

'Not that I could see,' said Mrs Kent. 'The police thought they must have panicked and run away after they shot Mr Arthur.'

Curiouser and curiouser, thought Justice. She wished she knew more about guns. Had Mr Arthur been killed with a single shot, and how difficult would this be to do?

Mrs Kent led Justice to a room she had never seen before. It must have been at the foot of the lighthouse tower because it was completely round, with narrow windows and specially-made bookcases around the curving walls.

'This was Mr Arthur's study,' she said. 'I've put out a few things for you to choose from. Can I offer you a cup of tea, Miss Morris?'

Justice was glad that the teacher accepted and the two women went away, leaving her alone in the beautiful circular room. The desk looked as if Mr Arthur had just left it. His pipe was there, as well as a notebook and several pens. How could he write in the notebook if he couldn't see? And why would a blind man have all these books? Maybe some of them were in the special raised print that blind people could decipher with their fingers. What was it called? Braille, that was it.

A few ornaments had also been placed on the desk – a bronze Alsatian, a wooden cat and a paperweight in the shape of an aeroplane – but Justice was more interested in the parts of the room that she wasn't supposed to explore. The desk drawers were locked but, in a wooden box with the initials FWA carved on the lid, she found a key. She felt a momentary twinge of conscience at the thought of looking at Mr Arthur's private things but then she remembered the last thing that he had ever said to her. *Remember, you are a detective and detectives never give up.*

The first drawer contained only official-looking letters. The second had a tin box with five interlocking rings on the lid. Justice opened it and found two medals inside, one gold and one bronze. Were they war medals? But the interlocking rings seemed familiar somehow. Oh yes, the Olympic Games. They had been held in Berlin last year and Justice's father had got very angry because the German Chancellor,

Adolf Hitler, had tried to stop Jewish people taking part. Were these Olympic medals? Could they have been won by Mr Arthur? But she had no time to dwell on possibilities. Mrs Kent and Miss Morris could be back at any minute. She opened the third drawer and found an envelope containing photographs. Justice looked through them quickly. Right at the bottom was a picture of a man who could only be a young Mr Arthur. He was in uniform and standing by a plane. Justice looked at the uniform and at the markings on the plane and she knew at once why there had been no mention of Mr Arthur in the records of the British Royal Flying Corps.

Mr Arthur had been a pilot.

In the German Air Force.

CHAPTER 15

Justice heard footsteps outside. Quickly she shut the drawer, locked it and put the key back in the box. When Mrs Kent opened the door, Justice was holding the bronze Alsatian.

'Could I possibly have this?' she said. 'It will remind me of Sabre.'

'Of course,' said Mrs Kent. 'Justice, Miss Morris said that you have to be getting back to the school but I have put some little cakes in a bag for you. Maybe you can share them with your friends?'

'Thank you very much,' said Justice. She could see another midnight feast coming up.

They said goodbye and scrunched away over the pebbles. Justice took one last look at the white house with the tower at one end. She remembered Dorothy's father saying that it had been a lighthouse once and, now she knew that, it seemed obvious. Smugglers' Lodge didn't look so sinister in the spring sunlight, with the seagulls calling above and the waves breaking against the shingle bar, but Justice remembered how it had looked at night, with the wind howling from the sea and the single light shining in the old lighthouse. *This is a house of secrets*, that's what Mr Arthur had said. Well, Justice probably wouldn't get a chance to find them out. She didn't think that she'd ever go inside Smugglers' Lodge again. But she didn't have time to feel sad – Miss Morris was walking fast and Justice had to jog to keep up with her.

The car was parked by a row of cottages. Justice thought that they were owned by fishermen because a few had lobster pots and nets by the door. But, as they approached, one of the front doors opened and a man came out with an Alsatian on a lead. It had to be Perkins, Mr Arthur's chauffeur, with Sabre. When he saw them Sabre wagged his tail and strained towards Justice. She almost thought that she could see him smiling.

'Miss Morris,' said Justice. 'That's Sabre. Can I say hallo?'

'Very well,' said Miss Morris. 'Just for a minute.' But she smiled pleasantly at Perkins and even patted Sabre, who extended a paw as if he was shaking hands.

Justice stroked the dog. She'd never been able to do this before because Sabre had always been on duty. She wondered what would happen to him now.

'I'll keep him with me,' said Perkins. 'But I'm worried he'll be bored. He's a working dog. And he misses his master.'

Sabre let out a small whine.

'He knows just what we're saying,' said Perkins, echoing Mrs Kent earlier. 'He's a smart one and no mistake.'

'I'll miss him,' said Justice. 'I'll miss Mr Arthur.' Her voice broke and she found that she couldn't say any more.

'He enjoyed your visits,' said Perkins. 'They really seemed to cheer him up. Before you started coming he just used to sit in that chair, looking out of the window – although he couldn't see anything. But, after he met you, he started to get his affairs in order. Just on the morning of the day he died, he'd seen his accountant and his solicitor. It was as if he was taking an interest in life again.'

And then he was killed, thought Justice. Shot as he sat in his favourite armchair. It was so unfair. Her eyes filled with tears. Perkins patted her on the shoulder and Sabre rubbed his head against her arm.

'Come on, Justice,' said Miss Morris, not unkindly. 'Time to be getting back to school.'

At Highbury House, Stella was waiting for her by the entrance to the dining hall.

'How was it?' she said.

'Sad,' said Justice. 'But I've found some things out. I'll tell you later.'

'Go into lunch, Justice and Stella,' said Miss Morris, appearing behind them. 'I want you to have your wits about you for this afternoon. I thought I might give the class a nice little maths test.'

Justice and Stella groaned. Only a teacher could describe a maths test as 'nice'.

They joined the other Barnowls at their usual table. The dining room was buzzing with voices as usual and, for once, Justice found the sound quite soothing.

'You missed Latin dictation this morning,' said Rose, cutting the gristle from her pork chop. 'You get all the luck.'

'She was at a funeral,' said Stella. 'That's not very lucky.'

'But she didn't know him very well,' said Rose, as if Justice was not there. 'It's not as if he was a family member.'

Justice considered bursting into tears just to make Rose feel bad but it felt like too much bother. Instead she said,

'Miss Morris is giving us a maths test this afternoon. She just told me.'

The girls all groaned. 'Oh, no,' said Eva, 'I hope it's not fractions. I never know what to do with them. Those silly little numbers balancing on top of each other.' Justice believed her; Eva had got one out of fifty in their last test.

'We've got cross-country tonight,' Rose told Justice. 'Don't forget.'

'I won't,' said Justice. 'Miss Heron was at the funeral.'

'Oh, you are lucky,' said Eva. 'You got to spend time with her.' The second years all still loved Miss Heron, even though she insisted on making them go on runs.

'Well, it was a funeral,' said Justice. 'We didn't spend much time chatting.'

She wondered about telling them that Miss Robinson had been there too and that her presence was clearly a surprise to the other teachers, but she decided to save this for Stella and Dorothy.

'I went back to Mr Arthur's house afterwards,' she said. 'His housekeeper gave me this as a keepsake.'

She got out the bronze Alsatian, which had been in the paper bag with the cakes. She wiped some cream off his nose and the girls leant forward to look.

'That's lovely,' said Nora. 'Makes me think of my dog, Barney, at home.'

'How sweet,' said Eva.

But, at the prefects' table, Helena Bliss was, like a magpie, drawn to the gleam of gold. She swooped over to the Barnowls.

'What's that, Justice? You can't have trinkets at the dining table.'

That was a new one. Justice suspected Helena of making up school rules as she went along. 'It's a present from a dead man,' she said. 'Miss Morris knows about it.'

Helena gave her a narrow look. 'Take it back to your dormy after lunch,' she said. 'And don't let me see it again.'

'I won't,' said Justice.

But Helena's command actually suited her just fine. As soon as they had finished their sponge pudding, Justice and Stella escaped to the dormy. Justice put the cakes and the ornament in her locker.

'We can have a midnight feast tonight,' she said. 'But I've got something else to tell you.' She told Stella about her discoveries at Smugglers' Lodge. Justice often thought that Stella didn't get excited enough about mysteries but now she listened to Justice's story with her hand over her mouth.

'Do you really think that someone broke in and deliberately killed Mr Arthur?'

'Yes,' said Justice. 'And we've got to find out why. I think I know why Mr Arthur didn't approach his daughter directly.' She told Stella about the photograph of Mr Arthur in German uniform.

'Mr Arthur was German?' said Stella. 'But he didn't have a foreign accent, did he?'

'He did have a slight accent, now I come to think of it,' said Justice. 'I just thought he had an unusual voice. And, of course, he'd spent a long time in England. He got married and had a child here. That explains why he had to go away during the war, of course. Maybe it explains why his wife divorced him and why his daughter won't see him.' She thought again of the unfinished line in the letter, *I know that you might think of me as an enemy* . . .

'That's so sad,' said Stella.

'Yes,' said Justice. 'My father said that the English pilots really admired the German ones. He says we shouldn't hold grudges now that the war is over.'

'At least there'll never be another war,' said Stella.

Justice didn't tell her friend that her father thought another war extremely likely. She said, 'I think there's something very suspicious about Mr Arthur's death. Why would a burglar shoot him and then not steal anything? And who would want to kill Mr Arthur? And isn't it suspicious that Mr Arthur was killed just when he was searching for his long-lost daughter?'

'We have to find Bunny now,' said Justice. 'It'll be a tribute to Mr Arthur.'

A voice from the doorway made them both jump. 'Justice. Stella. What are you doing here?'

It was Miss Robinson, in her nurse's uniform, a bunch of keys in her hand.

'Just putting something in my locker,' said Justice.

'You shouldn't be up here during the daytime,' said Miss Robinson. 'Go back downstairs. Afternoon lessons will be starting in a minute.'

The old matron would definitely have given them an order mark, so Justice and Stella were quick to obey. Even so, Justice couldn't help wondering just how much the new matron had overheard.

CHAPTER 16

Telling Stella wasn't enough. Justice wanted to share her suspicions with Dorothy too. She decided on another late-night visit.

After lights out, the Barnowls shared the cakes from Mrs Kent. They were delicious and disappeared in minutes. They chatted for a little while, sitting on the floor wrapped in blankets, but, when Miss Robinson's footsteps were heard outside, they jumped back into bed. Justice was very tired. After lessons, the cross-country team had been on an evening run with Miss Heron. They'd actually left the school grounds and jogged all the way to the village crossroads. Then, on the way back, Miss Heron had made them sprint the last hundred yards. It was some satisfaction to Justice that she'd come second to Moira, beating Rose by quite a distance.

But now her legs ached and she just wanted to close her eyes. The murder trials began to merge together in her head.

Rex v Stanley

Rex v Donagh and West

Rex v . . .

Rex. Rex. Rex was a dog's name. Sabre. Mr Arthur. *German Shepherds are very intelligent dogs. Remember, you are a detective and detectives never give up.*

Rex v Stanley

Justice jerked her head up. By the light of her torch she consulted her watch. Ten-thirty. She'd have to risk it. If she was going to see Dorothy, she had to do it now. Justice got out of bed and put on her slippers and dressing gown, then she tiptoed to the door. No sound from any of the beds, even Eva's. Justice slipped out and made her way along the corridor, careful not to step on the loose floorboards. There was a light at the end of the passage which must mean that Matron was still up. Hopefully she was reading medical textbooks or something equally exciting and wouldn't decide to venture out. Justice eased open the door to the landing. Then she froze. Another door was opening. Sick bay. Miss Robinson must be starting her rounds again. *Don't come this way*, Justice prayed.

It seemed as if her prayer was answered because she heard the click of a latch and then footsteps descending the staircase. Why was Miss Robinson going downstairs in the middle of the night? She'd been going the same way the last time Justice had seen her, when she was sneaking back from Dorothy's room at midnight. She remembered what Dad had said in his letter: *Watch out for the new matron, Miss Robinson. I think that there might be some mystery about her.* Really, it was almost her *duty* to follow. Justice crossed the landing and started down the stairs.

She paused every few minutes, just to give Miss Robinson time to stay ahead. She could hear the grandfather clock ticking in the great hall and the sound of a fox calling somewhere in the grounds. When Miss Robinson reached the ground floor she turned towards the assembly hall. Was she going into the basement again? Justice followed, slippers in hand so that her feet wouldn't make a noise. She watched from the shadows as Miss Robinson walked quickly across the room and opened the door that led to the basement. She left it slightly ajar. Did that mean that she was planning to come back the same way? As Justice recalled it, the only other way into the basement was through the kitchens. Did

Justice dare follow? But, if she didn't, how would she ever find the answer to the mystery? *Come on Justice*, she told herself, *screw your courage to the sticking place*. That was something Mum used to say.

Justice ran lightly across the room and began to descend the steps. It was very dark and she almost missed her footing at the bottom. She had her torch with her but didn't dare put it on. Was Miss Robinson still in the basement? Justice could no longer hear her footsteps. She edged along the passageway, feeling the brick wall at her back. Was she going to find out why the underground rooms were so strictly out of bounds this year?

Then she heard something. A skittering, scampering noise, very close by. Was it a mouse? There were lots of mice in the school because Mrs Hopkirk's cat, Rudi, was too lazy to catch them. Justice turned.

And then darkness descended.

CHAPTER 17

'Where am I?'

Miss Robinson was looking down at her. Justice could see the white uniform with the watch attached to the front pocket. Everything else seemed vague and indistinct, colours merging and blurring, sounds and voices just out of reach.

'In sick bay,' said Miss Robinson. 'Lie still. I think you might have concussion.'

Someone had said those words to her once before. Justice tried to sit up. 'How did I get here? I was . . .' Memories of dank, brick walls swirled around her brain. 'In . . . the basement.'

'The basement?' said Miss Robinson, her brow creasing. 'You weren't in the basement. Hutchins was doing his night rounds and he found you on the stage in the assembly hall. He carried you back up here.'

Justice was dimly aware of the large shape of the handyman in the background. 'The assembly hall?' she said.

'You've been sleepwalking,' said Miss Robinson. 'The funeral yesterday must have been a great strain on you, bringing back memories of . . . Well, bringing back all sorts of memories. The best thing you can do now is lie still. I've given you something to help you sleep.'

This rang a faint note of alarm in Justice's brain but, before she could do anything about it, she was asleep. When she woke up it was light outside. She was lying in bed in the sick bay, with a crisp, white sheet over her. Matron was sitting nearby, writing notes on a pad. She must have realised Justice was awake because she looked round.

'Ah, I'm glad you've come to. How are you feeling?'

'All right, I think,' said Justice. 'My head hurts a bit.'

'No wonder,' said Miss Robinson. 'You must have hit it quite hard when you fell over.' She sounded really sympathetic – but she could just be a good actress.

'Matron?' said Justice. 'Was I really in the assembly hall?'

'Yes,' said Miss Robinson. 'Hutchins found you lying in the middle of the stage. I think, subconsciously, you must have been worrying about that play and that's why you went there. The mind can play tricks on us. I learnt that when I was a nurse in the war. I've seen men who swore that they saw fiery angels, ten feet high, or the ghosts of dead comrades walking beside them.'

Justice's mind was working fast, making her head ache even more. She *had* been in the basement and, what's more, she had been following Miss Robinson. Why was the matron lying? And had she really been a nurse in the war? It sounded convincing enough but what about Ada's broken ankle, that Miss Robinson seemed to overlook? But the sleepwalking story was useful because it got Justice out of trouble. She wondered what Miss de Vere would say when she heard.

She didn't have to wonder long. After bringing Justice a (delicious) breakfast of toast and tea, Miss Robinson left her to read quietly. She'd only got a few pages into her Leslie Light book, *Murder in the Library*, when Miss de Vere appeared in the doorway.

'Are you feeling better, Justice?'

'Yes, Miss de Vere.'

The headmistress sat in the chair by the bed.

'Miss Robinson tells me that you were sleepwalking last night.'

'Yes, Miss de Vere. I don't remember anything about it.' This seemed the safest thing to say.

Miss de Vere gave her one of her sharp looks, the kind that seemed to see right into your mind. 'Miss Robinson thinks that you might have been upset by Mr Arthur's funeral. That it might have brought back memories of your mother.'

'It did make me think about her,' said Justice. Which was true.

The headmistress's expression softened slightly. 'It must have been hard for you. Rest here quietly today. You are excused lessons.'

'Thank you, Miss de Vere.'

'But, Justice . . .' The headmistress leant over the bed. 'If, by any chance, you weren't sleepwalking, if you were prowling around the house – or the basement – trying to solve some invented mystery, then I advise you to desist immediately. If you're discovered out of bounds again, then I'll start to be very suspicious about this "sleepwalking". Do you understand?'

'Yes, Miss de Vere. Can I ask a question?'

Miss de Vere smiled thinly. 'The two things you will

never be short of, Justice, are nerve and questions. Very well, I will allow one question.'

'Why is the basement out of bounds this term?'

'It is always out of bounds,' said Miss de Vere. 'But there was some subsidence during the holidays which has made the cellars unsafe. Does that answer your question?'

'Yes, Miss de Vere,' said Justice.

But, of course, it raised a whole lot of new questions. What was subsidence? Wasn't it when the ground itself moved? Why was that happening in the basement at Highbury House? And, if the cellars were so unsafe, why had Miss Robinson *and* Miss Hunting been seen there recently? But Justice didn't say any of this to the headmistress and, with another kindly admonition for Justice to look after herself, Miss de Vere left.

Justice's next visitor was far more welcome.

'Hallo,' said Dorothy from the doorway. 'Can I come in?'

'Of course!' said Justice. 'I was hoping I might see you.'

'I'm meant to be sweeping the upstairs corridors.' Dorothy brandished a broom. 'I'm safe for a few minutes.'

'I was coming to see you last night,' said Justice, 'but then I got distracted.'

She told Dorothy about the funeral and her discovery about Mr Arthur. She told her about following Miss Robinson into the basement last night and about waking up to find herself in sick bay with Miss Robinson bending over her, talking about sleepwalking.

'But I was in the basement,' said Justice. 'I remember it and, besides, look at my dressing gown.' It was hanging on the back of the door and the back was grey with dust.

'The only place it's that dusty is in the cellars,' said Justice.

'I know,' said Dorothy. 'I'm the one that does the dusting everywhere else.'

'There's something going on,' said Justice. 'Why is everyone going into the basement, especially if it's meant to be unsafe? What was Miss Robinson doing there in the middle of the night?'

'There must be some secret . . .' Dorothy began, and then she clutched Justice's arm. 'Justice! Remember what Dad said? There are meant to be tunnels going from Smugglers' Lodge to Highbury House. Where would the entrance to the tunnel be? In the basement!'

'Yes!' said Justice, sitting up in excitement. 'And if there was subsidence in the holidays, maybe that exposed the entrance of the tunnel? Now we just need to work out why

Miss Robinson and Miss Hunting were there. Were they trying to get to Smugglers' Lodge? And, if so, why?'

'Glad to hear that you're feeling better, Justice,' said a voice in the doorway. It was Miss Heron, dressed in her divided skirt and running shoes. Was she wearing them so that she could sneak up on them unnoticed?

'I'm feeling fine,' said Justice. Then, realising that this might mean that she had to go back to lessons, 'I mean, my head still hurts but I'm getting better.'

'You should be lying still and not gossiping,' said Miss Heron. 'We're having another evening run tomorrow. We're going to run across the marsh to the sea. I want you to be well enough to take part. I'm organising a cross-country competition against a few other schools for the last day of term. We need all the practice we can get.'

'I'll be well enough,' said Justice.

'Excellent,' said Miss Heron. 'Now, run along, Dorothy. I'm sure you've got work to do.'

CHAPTER 18

The next day was cold and misty.

'We'll get lost if we go running in this,' said Stella, looking out of the dormy window in the morning.

This triggered a memory in Justice's brain. Years ago, a pupil at Highbury House had got lost while running in a fog. The girl had fallen into a ditch and died there. Justice looked at Stella and knew that she was remembering the same thing.

'The mist will clear,' said Rose. 'It always does. I don't expect you'll be able to run very fast, Justice, what with your terrible injury and all that.'

According to Stella, Justice's sleepwalking was the talk of the school. In some versions she'd been left for dead, after being attacked by an unknown assailant. In others, she'd been found on the stage, acting the part of Lady Macbeth while in a trance.

'I'll cope,' said Justice. 'It would be awful if I beat you, even after my head injury, wouldn't it?'

Rose scowled and Eva hastily reminded them that it was time for breakfast. 'I bet it'll be super,' she added, almost as if she'd never tasted a Highbury House meal.

The fog did clear as the day went on. Miss Robinson asked to see Justice at first break, just to 'check up on her'. Justice wasn't sure if she trusted the matron. At the least, she was a somewhat slapdash nurse, at the worst she was a sinister figure who had been in the basement last night and then lied about it. But Justice did want to go on the run and said as much.

'Where are you planning to go?' asked Miss Robinson.

'To the sea, Miss Heron said.'

'You should be fine,' said Miss Robinson. 'Just don't take it too fast.'

That showed how much Miss Robinson knew about running. The whole point was to set a good time. But at least Justice could join her teammates.

At lunchtime Miss Heron came over to tell Rose, Justice and Stella to be ready at the school gates at five. She would arrange for them to have meal early. Then she went to the Doves' table to pass on the news to Alicia and Moira.

'Hope you don't see the Headless Horseman,' said Nora brightly.

'Don't tell me there's another ghost hanging about the place,' said Justice.

'Oh, yes.' Nora adjusted her spectacles. 'The Headless Horseman of the marshes. You hear horses' hooves, you turn round and there's nothing there but, when you turn back, the horseman is beside you, grinning at you.'

'How can he grin without a head?' said Justice.

'He's holding it in his hand,' said Nora, 'dripping blood.'

Eva gave a little scream. 'Don't, Nora! I'll have nightmares tonight.'

'Nora's talking rubbish as usual,' said Rose. 'Pass the salt, please. This spam tastes like rubber.'

But, as they waited by the gates with the stone griffins on either side, there *was* something slightly spooky about the evening. It wasn't quite dark yet but the shadows were lengthening and a faint wind was making the trees whisper and rustle. The girls stood very close together as they waited for Miss Heron. Tiny wisps of fog were blowing like smoke across the marshes. Justice thought again of her first view of Highbury House and the note that she'd written in her journal. *Chance of escape without being seen: minimal. Potential for murder: high.*

Miss Heron seemed to appear from nowhere, glowing slightly in her white cricket jumper. Justice wished that they all had bright clothes on but the girls were in their brown jumpers and gym skirts. If a fog came down, they would vanish into the gloom.

'Come on, girls,' said Miss Heron. 'We're going to run to the sea and back again. We'll need to move fast if we want to be back by nightfall.'

'To the sea?' said Rose. 'But that's miles.'

'No, it's not,' said Miss Heron. 'I checked the route this morning. It's half an hour there and half an hour back.'

'Do you know this area well, Miss Heron?' asked Justice, seeing the chance to get some sleuthing done. 'Were you brought up on the Romney Marsh?'

Miss Heron gave her a sharp look. 'No,' she said. 'I simply believe in getting to know the local terrain. Now, let's go.'

They set off, running in single file, following Miss Heron in her white jumper. Justice was between Moira and Alicia but, after about ten minutes, Rose moved up to run beside Alicia, and Stella caught up with Justice. They didn't speak because Miss Heron was setting a fast pace. Justice could feel her heart pumping and her lungs burning, but all that practice must be paying off because she found that she could keep going. And it was comforting to have her friend beside her. Despite herself, she thought of Nora's story. *You hear horses' hooves, you turn round and there's nothing there but, when you turn back, the horseman is beside you, grinning at you.* Funny how your mind played tricks. From the time they had left the school, Justice had the strangest feeling that someone was following them. Now she could almost swear that she could hear horses' hooves, relentless, pursuing, the fateful sound getting nearer and nearer. She heard Rose give a slight scream and she swung round, almost expecting to see the severed head with its evil grin.

Instead she saw a farmer's cart pulled by a dappled horse. The lantern at the front cast an eerie, fragmented light. Justice realised that night had almost fallen.

'Are you from the school?' shouted a man's voice.

'Yes,' said Miss Heron. 'We're going for a run.'

'Best go back,' said the man. 'Fog's coming down.'

'We're not going far,' said Miss Heron. 'Just to the coast and back.'

'You'd best be quick,' said the man. 'And watch out for the lights.'

'What lights?' said Justice. She knew that she wasn't meant to speak directly to adults with a teacher present but she couldn't help herself.

'There are strange lights on the marshes at night,' said the man. 'The devils' lights, folk round here call them.'

Justice thought of the green haze that she sometimes saw on the horizon late at night. Phosphorescence, said Miss Loomis, their science teacher. Marsh gas. But maybe they were the devils' lights. She thought of the wreckers' lights, leading the sailors to their deaths. *The wreckers, they used to call them. They'd shine lanterns along the coast path, where the sandbars were. The ships would crash and the wreckers would steal everything on board. Wicked, I call it. Lots of the poor sailors drowned . . .*

'If you follow the lights and leave the path,' said the man, 'then you're lost.'

Lost. It sounded worse than losing your way. It sounded as if you could be lost for ever.

'Let's go back,' said Rose.

'No,' said Miss Heron. 'It's just a step further. We need a proper practice run. Thank you,' she said to the man, with a clear note of dismissal in her voice.

'Evening,' the man said. Then he spoke to his horse and the cart started forward. Justice watched the lantern light disappearing, feeling as if all their security was going with it. It was much darker now and she could only just see Miss Heron's jumper.

'Come on, girls.' They started running again. Soon Justice could smell the sea, that stinging, briny scent that reminded her of collecting shells with her dad. Then they could hear it, the waves crashing against the shingle. Miss Heron called a halt and handed out sweets. 'Glucose,' she said. 'For energy.'

Justice didn't much like sweets but this one tasted delicious. She looked out to where the sea should be but there was only blackness with the occasional white crest of a wave. They were on the edge of the sand dunes and, in the distance, along the curve of the bay, she could see a single light shining. Smugglers' Lodge.

The girls were sitting on the coarse grass at the top of the dunes, sucking their sweets and gazing out at the dark water. 'We'd better get going,' said Miss Heron. 'I want to be back at the school by six.' Then Justice heard her give an exclamation of alarm. Justice turned.

The fog had come down. As swiftly and silently as if a curtain had fallen, there was now a thick mist between them and the land.

Rose started to cry. 'We're trapped,' she said. 'We'll never get back. That old man in the cart was right. We'll be lost for ever.'

'Don't be silly,' said Miss Heron. Justice couldn't see her face but she thought that the games mistress sounded anxious all the same.

'I've got a torch,' said Justice. She always carried it when she went anywhere at night. She shone it in the direction of the marshes but the beam of light only reflected the fog back at them, the tiny motes dancing in the air.

'What shall we do?' said Moira, her usually no-nonsense, Scots voice sounding faint and quavery.

'We'll have to go along the coastal path,' said Miss Heron. 'It leads to the village. When we get there I'll find somewhere where I can telephone for Hutchins to come and get us.'

'That's Smugglers' Lodge,' said Justice, pointing to the light on the other side of the bay. 'We can telephone from the house.'

'Smugglers' Lodge?' said Rose. 'We can't go there. It's haunted. I heard you telling Stella.'

'Those are just stories,' said Justice, hoping that this was the truth. 'It's a nice house and the housekeeper, Mrs Kent, is very kind. She'll give us hot chocolate and biscuits.'

She could sense the girls cheering up at this. 'Very well,' said Miss Heron, after a moment's thought. 'Let's head for Smugglers' Lodge. Follow the light, girls.'

It was only after they had set off that Justice remembered the farmer's warning. *If you follow the lights and leave the path, then you're lost.*

* * *

It grew darker and darker as they jogged along the path. Justice led the way with her torch and Miss Heron brought up the rear. They could hear the waves getting stronger as the wind picked up and occasionally they could feel the sea-spray against their faces. Stella was next to Justice and, once again, Justice was glad of her friend's stalwart presence. Behind them Rose was whimpering as she ran – occasionally Justice heard the words 'my parents' and 'not fair'. For a while it seemed as if Smugglers' Lodge was never going to get any closer but then, quite suddenly, the white house was above them with the light shining high in the tower. *Why aren't there any lights on the lower floor?* thought Justice. *What if Mrs Kent has already left?* She was exhausted by now, her face wet with salt water and her shoes leaking. She was sure that the other girls were all in the same state. Alicia had fallen on some uneven ground and hurt her ankle. She was having to be supported by Moira and Miss Heron. They needed to get inside quickly.

Justice ran up the steps and pounded the brass anchor on the door. She thought of her other visits, when Sabre had often barked before she had time to knock. But Sabre was living with Perkins now.

Thank goodness there were footsteps on the other side of the door. Then it was opened and the tall figure of Mrs Kent stood silhouetted against the light.

'Justice! Whatever are you doing here?'

'Please . . . we went running and then the fog came down . . . there are five of us and our teacher.'

'Come in,' said the housekeeper. 'It's not a night to be outside. Come in and get dry.'

The girls didn't need telling twice. They practically fell over the doorstep and, before long, they were installed in the kitchen with towels to dry their hair and steaming cups of hot chocolate in front of them.

'Can I telephone the school?' Miss Heron asked. 'I don't think the girls could stand the walk back. Alicia here has sprained her ankle badly.'

Alicia's ankle was swollen and she looked very pale. Moira had a cut on her cheek and Rose appeared ready to have hysterics.

Mrs Kent looked worried. 'Oh, I'm sorry, we don't have a telephone line here. Mr Arthur was something of a recluse, you see.'

Rose started to cry.

'I'll have to go into the village,' said Miss Heron. 'You stay here, girls. I won't be long.'

'Let me lend you a raincoat,' said Mrs Kent. 'There's a storm coming.'

CHAPTER 19

'I haven't got much food in,' said Mrs Kent. 'But I can make you all some cheese on toast if you're hungry.'

The girls agreed fervently that they were hungry. It seemed years since they'd eaten meal, alone in the refectory. It was quite cosy, sitting around the scrubbed table in Mr Arthur's kitchen while the wind howled outside. Mrs Kent put slices of bread under the grill and Stella and Moira jumped up to lay the table. Rose sat sulkily in the corner and Alicia had her foot raised up on a stool. Normally Justice would have helped but she felt strangely uneasy. The storm outside sounded wilder and wilder; she could hear the waves too, crashing against the shingle bar only a few feet away. It felt odd to be in the house without Mr Arthur and Sabre. The kitchen was warm and brightly lit but she was conscious of all the rooms above them, Mr Arthur's study lying empty with his pipe and notebook on the desk, the deserted lighthouse with the light still shining.

'Mrs Kent?' she said. 'Why is there a light in the tower?'

Mrs Kent was putting cheese on the bread. She turned and smiled. 'It was something Mr Arthur liked to do. He said that the lighthouse was a beacon in the darkness, showing sailors a safe way in to port. "Maybe some wanderer will see our light," he used to say, "and find the way home." I always light it now in his memory.'

'We saw the light,' said Justice. 'It saved us.' She wondered whether Mr Arthur had been thinking about his daughter when he talked about the light showing wanderers the way home. It seemed so sad that he'd never been reunited with his only child.

The toasted cheese was delicious and Mrs Kent made them more hot chocolate to have with it. Afterwards there were scones and slices of fruit cake. The girls became quite cheerful, laughing about their run over the marshes and about the sinister man in the cart.

'Don't follow the lights,' said Moira, in what was obviously meant to be a Kentish accent, 'they'll lead you to your death.' She cackled horribly and helped herself to another piece of cake.

'I thought he was the headless horseman,' said Stella. 'I didn't want to turn round in case he threw his head at me.'

'I wasn't scared,' said Rose, tossing back her hair.

'We were all scared,' said Stella, 'even Justice, and she's the bravest person I know.'

Justice didn't like to say so, but she was still scared. The storm was howling outside, rattling the windows, and she wondered why no one else was asking the question that was screaming in her head.

Where was Miss Heron?

Mrs Kent left them eating cake. 'I have to check that the windows are secured,' she said. 'The wind's getting up.' Justice looked at the kitchen windows, covered by bright yellow curtains. Was this where the burglars had broken in? If so, there was no trace of it now.

'Come on,' she whispered to Stella. 'Let's explore a bit.'

Stella raised her eyebrows but she followed Justice out of the room, muttering something about 'finding the loo'.

'What are we looking for?' she said.

'The answer to the mystery,' said Justice briskly. She wasn't sure which mystery she meant. It was all bound together in some way: the long-lost daughter, the basement, Miss Robinson's odd behaviour, the gunshot in the night.

'We need to find Mr Arthur's study,' she said. It had been in the bottom of the tower, and the walls had been different – brick instead of white plaster. Yes, this was right. Down two steps and along a corridor with pictures of planes. This was the door. It would probably be locked but it was worth a try.

The door wasn't locked but, when Justice stepped inside the room, a far nastier surprise awaited her.

Miss Robinson, holding a gun.

Stella gave a scream. Justice grabbed her hand and the two girls started backing away.

'Hallo, Justice,' said Miss Robinson, as if they were meeting in the dormy or in sick bay.

'What are you doing here?' said Justice.

'Just doing my job,' said Miss Robinson, still holding the gun in what looked like a very professional way. It was a black pistol, snub-nosed and small enough to fit in a pocket or a nurse's bag.

'Your job?' said Justice. 'But you're a nurse. You're *Matron*.'

Miss Robinson laughed. 'I'm no nurse. Now, get out of my way, girls. I've work to do.'

She stepped towards them. Justice and Stella backed away still further but, as they did so, Justice saw something that made her eyes almost pop out of her head. One of the bookcases was opening. A dark rectangle appeared and, in the middle of it, the figure of a girl. Dorothy. Quick as a flash, Dorothy took in the situation, picked up a brass model of a plane and hit Miss Robinson over the head.

The woman went down like a felled tree.

'You've killed her,' said Stella, her voice rising hysterically.

'She's just knocked out,' said Dorothy, sounding rather breathless.

'Dorothy!' said Justice. 'How did you get here?'

'I found the secret passage,' said Dorothy. 'I saw Miss Robinson going into the basement and followed her. It leads all the way here. Isn't it exciting?'

'Exciting?' said Stella. 'It's terrifying. Are you sure Matron isn't dead?'

Justice knelt down beside the body. She picked up Miss Robinson's limp hand and felt a pulse beneath her fingers. 'She's still breathing,' she said. 'What was she doing here? And why did she have a gun? Looks like you were right about her not being a nurse, Dorothy.'

'What's going on?' said a voice from the doorway. The girls turned to see Mrs Kent standing there, wearing a hat and a voluminous raincoat. The housekeeper took in the woman on the floor, the gun a few feet away and the opening in the bookcase.

She acted with admirable calm. She knelt beside Miss Robinson's body. 'Who's this?' she said.

'The matron at our school,' said Justice. She thought that this was the easiest explanation.

'I'm Dorothy,' said Dorothy brightly.

'How did you get here?' said Mrs Kent, straightening up. Then, answering her own question, 'The secret passage. Mr Arthur thought the entrance might be here. Does it lead all the way from Highbury House?'

'Yes,' said Dorothy. 'It's ever such a long way but I think it has been used quite recently. There were footprints in the dust. Miss Robinson obviously knew the way to open this door from the inside. I think she'd been here before.'

Justice looked at the gun. Had Miss Robinson stolen through the passage and killed Mr Arthur? If so, why? Mrs Kent followed her gaze. 'I'll take that,' she said, and picked up the gun.

'Be careful,' said Justice. 'I think it's loaded.'

'Don't worry,' said Mrs Kent. 'I'm a countrywoman. I know about guns.'

She put the weapon in her pocket. 'Help me get this woman – Matron – on to the sofa, girls.'

Dorothy and Justice helped lift Miss Robinson on to the leather chesterfield. Then Mrs Kent covered her with a furry rug. Stella seemed turned to stone.

'Now,' said Mrs Kent. 'You girls go into the kitchen and stay there. I'm going to the village to get help. And I'm worried about your games mistress too. She ought to have been back by now.'

Don't go, Justice wanted to say. But the housekeeper was already halfway down the corridor. They heard her footsteps receding, then the front door opening and shutting. Then silence.

CHAPTER 20

'What's *she* doing here?' said Rose.

'Hallo, Rose,' said Dorothy. 'I came through a secret passage from Highbury House. Is that cake? Can I have a piece?'

Rose, Moira and Alicia stared as Dorothy took some cake and started to eat. Justice could tell that, for Rose, this was almost the most shocking thing that had happened that day. A *servant*, sitting and eating with them!

'The secret passage came out in Mr Arthur's study,' said Justice. 'Miss Robinson was there too. Dorothy knocked her out.'

'Miss Robinson?' said Rose. '*Matron?*'

'Actually, I don't think she really is Matron,' said Justice. 'Well, she is – but she's not a proper nurse. She had a gun, for one thing.'

'I think she was going to kill us,' said Stella. 'But Dorothy hit her over the head before she could explain why.'

'Where's the gun now?' asked Moira, fixing on the important point.

'Mrs Kent took it,' said Stella. 'She's gone to the village to get help.'

'Where's Miss Heron?' said Rose, as if noticing the teacher's absence for the first time.

'I don't know,' said Justice. 'She should have been back by now. The village is only ten minutes away. I've walked there from here loads of times.'

'What shall we do?' said Alicia. 'Where are all the grown-ups?'

Grown-ups don't always keep you safe, thought Justice. She remembered Miss Robinson pointing a gun at them. But she didn't think she should say this to Alicia. She was very pale after her accident and Justice was worried that she might faint.

'Mrs Kent said stay in here,' said Justice. 'I vote we barricade ourselves in. Miss Robinson might wake up at any time. She hasn't got her gun but I think she could still get pretty nasty.'

This spurred the cross-country team into action. There was a heavy bench by the table and they pushed it against the door.

'We should sit on the bench,' said Justice. 'That will make it harder to move.'

Justice, Stella, Dorothy and Rose sat in a line with their backs against the door. Alicia was opposite, still with her bad leg raised. Moira was opening the cutlery drawers.

'I'm looking for weapons,' she said. 'Bingo!' She brandished a rolling pin. 'We should be armed.' She handed Stella a copper ladle.

'Would you really be able to hit someone?' asked Stella.

'Och, I think so,' said Moira. 'If it was them or me.' She found two more ladles and gave them to Justice and Rose.

'What about me?' said Dorothy. 'I've already knocked someone out today.'

'So you have,' said Moira. 'Fair play to you.' She gave Dorothy something that looked like a wooden hammer.

'What's that?' said Rose.

'It's for hitting meat to make it tender,' said Dorothy. 'Haven't you seen one before?'

'I'm happy to say that I've hardly ever been in a kitchen,' said Rose, in her loftiest voice.

'I have,' said Stella. 'I often help my mother with the cooking.'

'So do I,' said Dorothy.

'Me too,' said Moira. 'We haven't got enough money to have a cook.'

Rose looked shocked. It was almost the first time any of the girls had admitted that they weren't as wealthy as her. Justice wished that she could join in but the truth was that she and Dad did have a 'daily' who cooked for them. *I'm probably as ignorant as Rose about domestic tasks*, she thought guiltily.

For some reason, though, this conversation seemed to bring them all closer. They took up their positions again, with their weapons/cooking utensils in their hands. The clock above the kitchen stove said ten o'clock. It felt like midnight. Outside the wind was still roaring, rattling the windows in their frames.

'What's that?' said Rose.

'What?' said Alicia.

'That noise.'

'It's just the wind,' said Moira.

'No, it's a sort of scrabbling. Listen.'

They listened. And, above the noise of the storm, Justice heard it. A scuffling, scratching noise and then a low moan.

Alicia screamed. 'It's a ghost!'

'It's the headless horseman,' said Rose.

'Rubbish,' said Justice, although the sound had made her blood run cold. She got up and moved towards the back door.

'Be careful, Justice,' said Stella.

The noise was getting louder. Now it was more of an insistent whine. Justice touched the door handle.

'What are you doing?' said Rose. 'Get away from the door!'

But Justice turned the key in the lock and opened the door. A dark shape bounded into the room. All the girls screamed.

'It's a wolf!' said Alicia. 'It's going to kill us.'

'No, I think it's a dog,' said Dorothy. 'A very big one.'

'Sabre!' Justice flung her arms round the Alsatian's neck. 'What are you doing here?'

The dog's fur was soaking but his tail was wagging. He looked at Justice as if to try to make her understand something.

'This is Mr Arthur's dog,' said Justice. 'He's meant to be living with the chauffeur in his cottage. I don't know what he's doing here.'

'Are you sure he's safe?' said Alicia. But Sabre was already making friends with Stella, Dorothy and Moira.

Even Rose deigned to pat him, although she wiped her hands on her skirt afterwards.

'Sabre knows there's some mystery,' said Justice. 'Look, I might as well tell you everything.'

They sat back down with Sabre next to Justice and she told the other girls about Mr Arthur, his missing daughter and his suspicious death.

'So his daughter could be one of the teachers at the school,' said Moira. 'It could be Miss Heron or Miss de Vere.'

'It's not Miss de Vere,' said Justice, 'because my dad's met her father. It could be Miss Heron or Miss Robinson. They've both been behaving very suspiciously and they were both at Mr Arthur's funeral. Or it could be Miss Hunting. I saw her in the basement the day I followed Miss Robinson down there.'

'But you said that Mr Arthur was German,' said Rose. 'They're not German.'

'His daughter was English,' said Justice. 'Mr Arthur lived here before the war. Anyway, Germans are just people like us. There's no difference.'

Rose looked as if she wanted to disagree. But before she could there was a loud knock on the door – the door behind which Matron was lying.

'Oh, no,' said Stella. 'It's Miss Robinson.' Moira raised her rolling pin.

Justice looked at Sabre. He had his head on one side but his tail was still wagging. 'Who is it?' she called.

'Miss Morris,' was the surprising answer. 'Open the door at once.'

They pulled the bench away from the door and opened it. Their form teacher stood there, grim-faced, in her usual tweeds. Justice noticed at once, though, that neither her hair nor her clothes were wet. Miss Morris must have come through the tunnel.

'Could someone please tell me what's going on?' said Miss Morris.

Six voices answered her.

'Cross-country run . . .'

'Fog . . .'

'Miss Robinson . . .'

'. . . had a gun . . .'

'Mrs Kent . . .'

'The storm . . .'

'Secret passage . . .'

'Quiet.' Miss Morris raised her hand. 'One at a time, please.'

Everyone looked at Justice. Sighing, she tried to give a brief account of everything that had happened once they had left the school gates.

Miss Morris listened intently, her eyes gleaming behind her little, gold glasses.

'I've just come through the passage,' she said. 'Miss Robinson wasn't in the room where it comes out, the round room with the bookcases.'

The girls looked at each other. That must mean that Miss Robinson was somewhere near, maybe still in the house. It was not a comfortable thought.

'How did you know about the secret passage?' asked Justice.

'All the senior teachers know,' said Miss Morris. 'Miss Hunting has been researching the history of the house for her book and she always suspected it was there. The subsidence exposed the entrance. But I had no idea how far back it went. When Miss Robinson didn't appear for her evening rounds, I went into the basement to check and saw footprints leading into the tunnel. Two sets, it appears. I presume that's how you got here, Dorothy?'

'Yes,' said Dorothy, looking rather abashed.

Justice's mind was racing. Why did Miss Morris check in the basement for Miss Robinson? Did that mean that she was suspicious of the new matron or that they were working together in some way? But why and what for?

Before Justice could ask any more questions, there was a

sound outside. Sabre gave a low growl. Moira raised the rolling pin again.

The back door opened. Justice must have forgotten to lock it. She looked round and was touched to see that Stella and Dorothy had come to stand on either side of her. She put a hand on Sabre's collar to give herself courage.

Two people staggered over the threshold: Mrs Kent, her raincoat slick with water, supporting a bedraggled-looking Miss Heron.

'Margaret!' said Miss Morris. 'What happened to you?'

Miss Heron looked up, in a rather dazed fashion. 'Edna? What are you doing here? I went to get help and I fell down the shingle bank. I hurt my arm and must have passed out. Mrs Kent has just come to my rescue.'

'I found her on the way back from the village,' said Mrs Kent, once more accepting the appearance of another stranger without comment. 'I think her arm may be broken.'

She helped the games mistress into a chair. Miss Heron's face was greenish white but she tried to smile.

'I need Miss Robinson to look at my arm,' she said.

'I don't think you do,' said Miss Morris dryly. 'It seems our new matron is not quite what she seems.'

'There's something very fishy about that woman,' said

175

Mrs Kent. 'I've seen her hanging around the house a few times.'

'She's escaped,' said Justice. 'Miss Morris came through the secret tunnel and Miss Robinson wasn't in the study any more.'

'I see,' said Mrs Kent. 'Well, the police are on their way. I managed to telephone from the public house.' She said the words with distaste.

'Thank goodness,' said Justice. But, looking up at Miss Morris, she thought that she saw a strange expression on her form teacher's face. Was it annoyance, or fear?

'We should all stay in the kitchen,' said Mrs Kent. 'I can lock us in until the police get here. That way we'll be safe from Miss Robinson.'

But will we? thought Justice. Miss Robinson might not have her gun but Justice thought that she could still do them some harm, if she put her mind to it. But why would Miss Robinson want to hurt them? It didn't make sense somehow. She realised that the housekeeper was talking to her. 'I'll fetch some blankets. Justice, will you give me a hand?'

Justice was honoured to be asked but she was also rather apprehensive at the thought of wandering about the house with Miss Robinson on the loose. She hoped that Sabre would come with them but Mrs Kent told him to stay and guard the others. Mrs Kent tried to distract the dog with some biscuits but Sabre wouldn't eat them. He kept looking at the door and whining. Eventually Miss Morris held on to the dog's collar to stop him following the housekeeper. But, when they left the kitchen, Justice saw that Dorothy was still at her side. She wasn't quite as good protection as an Alsatian, but she was the next best thing.

Mrs Kent led them along a stone passageway. She came to a small door and opened it. Justice held out her arms for the blankets. From the kitchen, she could hear Sabre barking.

In that second, she thought of several things:

The day he died, Mr Arthur had seen his solicitor.

Sabre had been fed poisoned meat.

Sabre had refused to eat the biscuits Mrs Kent gave him. He had growled when he heard her at the door.

Mr Arthur had been shot as he sat in his chair.

And she heard Mrs Kent saying, 'I'm a countrywoman. I know about guns.'

When she looked back at Mrs Kent, the housekeeper was pointing the gun at her.

'Get into the cupboard, Justice,' she said.

CHAPTER 21

'It was *you*,' said Justice. 'You killed Mr Arthur. Was it because he was going to change his will in favour of his daughter? He saw his solicitor the day he died, didn't he?'

'You are a very nosy little girl,' said Mrs Kent. 'I can't think what Mr Arthur saw in you.'

Justice turned, wondering if she could bolt back into the kitchen, but Mrs Kent gestured with the gun. 'I would hate there to be a tragic accident. Gun goes off accidentally, schoolgirl found dead. A schoolgirl *and* a maid.' She looked at Dorothy with something like contempt. 'Get into the cupboard, both of you. I'll deal with you later.'

There was nothing for it but to obey.

Mrs Kent slammed the door and turned the lock, leaving Justice and Dorothy in the darkness. But Justice was not an amateur sleuth for nothing. She still had her torch in her pocket. Its light picked out a tiny room with brick walls and ceiling and a stone floor.

'Let's shout,' said Dorothy. 'They might hear us from the kitchen.'

They yelled 'Help!' at the tops of their voices but, although they could still hear Sabre barking, no one came to rescue them.

'The storm's still really loud,' said Justice. 'They can't hear us. Sabre can but they won't know why he's barking.' She thought of Perkins saying, '*He knows just what we're saying.*' Sabre had known all along who had killed his master and he had tried to tell them, in his own way. That must have been why the dog had escaped from the chauffeur's house. Because he knew that something bad was happening at Smugglers' Lodge.

'Do you think Mrs Kent will kill us?' said Dorothy. She tried to sound brave but Justice could hear the wobble in her voice.

'No,' she said, though she wasn't at all sure. 'She just wants to keep us out of the way.'

'But she said she'd deal with us later.'

'That was just bluster,' blustered Justice. 'We have to try and escape though. We must get help. I don't believe Mrs Kent ever called the police. And there's Miss Robinson to contend with too.' She rattled the door but the solid wood didn't give way, even when the two of them pushed with all their might. Justice shone the torch round the room again. On one wall there was a dresser, the sort that you find in a kitchen with plates on it. Only this one was empty.

'What's that doing here?' she said.

'It's probably an old one,' said Dorothy. 'With woodworm or something.' She gave the shelves a nudge.

The dresser moved.

'Did you see that?' said Dorothy.

'Yes,' said Justice. 'Push again.'

They both pushed and slowly, creakily, the dresser moved back to reveal a black hole in the wall.

'It's another tunnel,' said Dorothy.

Justice shone her torch into the opening. She saw brick walls, green with what looked like moss, and stairs going down. She couldn't see the bottom and there was an unpleasant, damp smell.

'Where do you think it goes?' said Dorothy, leaning over her shoulder.

'To the village, I hope,' said Justice. 'Isn't that what your dad said? That most of the passages from Smugglers' Lodge lead to the village?'

'What if it's a dead end?'

'Well, we have to try,' said Justice, even though she dreaded descending those dark, clammy-looking steps. 'What choice do we have?'

Justice went first, shining her torch in front of her. Dorothy was behind her, so close that Justice could hear her breathing.

She tried to count the steps but gave up after thirty. And then, suddenly, they were on level ground. The floor was brick but the walls were rough, made of what looked like chalk. Justice reached out her hand and touched one. It was damp, like something that had been under water. The tunnel was narrow, they could touch its sides without extending their arms, but it was high enough that they didn't have to crouch. *At least Mrs Kent and Miss Robinson are both tall*, thought Justice. They'd find it more difficult. She was aware that they had left the dresser pushed back. It would be obvious where they had gone.

The tunnel seemed to go on for ever. Justice thought of all that earth above, pressing down on her. What if Mrs Kent came after them? There would be no escape in the narrow passageway. Justice tried to walk more quickly and was suddenly aware that the tunnel was going downwards. Then it turned sharply to the right. Justice stopped. This wasn't good. She had been hoping for an upward slope or even some stairs.

'Where are we going?' said Dorothy, close behind her, her voice sounding echoey and strange. 'I don't like it.'

'You came through that other tunnel all on your own,' said Justice.

'That wasn't such a tight fit,' said Dorothy. 'And I guessed that it must lead somewhere. This might be a dead end. We might be trapped here for ever.'

'We have to keep going,' said Justice. 'It's all we can do.'

She turned the corner and came face to face with a skeleton. Justice screamed. Dorothy cannoned into the back of her and then she screamed too. The skeleton was lying on the brick floor with one bony arm stretched out, as if it was desperately trying to claw its way out. Next to the horrible bones there was a wooden box, bound with iron bands. Justice opened it. The box was empty.

'Justice!' Dorothy's voice was a suppressed scream. 'You haven't got time to go looking in boxes. We have to find our way out. Or we'll be . . . or we'll die.'

Justice pointed her torch at the stone wall in front of her. *Please don't let it be a dead end.* For a moment, she thought it was, and then she saw metal rings set into the wall.

'We have to climb up,' she said. She put her torch between her teeth and reached for the first rung.

It was hard going. Justice had never got the hang of climbing the equipment in the school gymnasium and this was much more difficult. She thought of Miss Heron saying, *'It's not about being good at games. It's about being determined.'* She thought of the skeleton below who, presumably, had once been a human being like herself, trapped in this tunnel. She gritted her teeth and reached upwards, the rusty metal cutting into her hands. Then, just when she thought she couldn't climb any more, her head hit something solid.

'It's a trap door,' she said. She reached upwards and, in doing so, knocked the torch out of her mouth. She heard it crash on the brick floor.

They were in total darkness.

'My torch!' said Justice. She felt like crying. That torch had been her constant companion at Highbury House, a vital part of her survival kit.

'It doesn't matter,' said Dorothy, below her. 'Just try to open the hatch.'

'I am.' Justice pushed with all her might and, miraculously, the wood seemed to shift slightly. Justice heaved some more and then she felt the rain on her face. One more heave and her head was out in the open. She was immediately almost blinded by the rain, blown into her face by the wind. The storm was obviously still raging.

Justice hoisted herself out and turned to help Dorothy. Then they collapsed on the grass, oblivious to the wind and the rain. For a while they didn't speak but then Justice began to be aware of hazy moonlight, illuminating dark shapes around her – not houses but solid structures, square and somehow sinister.

'We're in the graveyard,' said Dorothy.

'The church,' said Justice. 'Your father said that the vicar used to be in league with the smugglers. They must have used this tunnel to move the goods into the church.'

'We're near my house then,' said Dorothy, her voice breaking with relief. 'We can go and get help. My mum and dad will be there. And John.'

'Not so fast,' said a voice that seemed to come out of the ground itself. Mrs Kent, gun in hand, was emerging from the tunnel.

'Run!' shouted Justice.

They hurtled between the gravestones. The moon had disappeared and the rain drove straight into their faces, making it almost impossible to see where they were going. The tombstones loomed up around them – angels, Madonnas and towering crosses. The jagged light from Mrs Kent's torch was following them. Justice hid behind one of the largest stones, pulling Dorothy after her. They waited, and Justice thought that she could hear her heart thumping. Then she realised that Dorothy was pointing towards a faint light in the distance. It must be coming from the cottages. The girls nodded at each other and started to run. Justice was almost at the gate when she heard a cry. Dorothy had fallen over one of the half-buried stones. Justice went back and pulled Dorothy to her feet but it was too late. Mrs Kent had caught up with them. The housekeeper levelled the gun. Justice could see it gleaming in the darkness.

Then a second shape appeared, a cloaked figure that seemed taller than any human. It threw itself on Mrs Kent and brought her to the ground in a rugby tackle. Then it took hold of the gun.

'Are you all right, girls?'

It was Miss Robinson, her nurse's cloak flying up in the wind. Justice and Dorothy stood staring, shivering and soaked to the skin.

'Yes,' said Justice, wondering if this was at all true. Mrs Kent might be on the ground but Miss Robinson, the gun's original owner, could easily shoot them.

'Go and get help,' said Miss Robinson. Then, to the figure at her feet, 'Beryl Kent, I'm arresting you for the murder of Friedrich Arthur and the attempted murder of Justice Jones and Dorothy Smith.'

'Are you a policewoman?' asked Justice.

'Private detective,' said Miss Robinson. 'This is a citizen's arrest. Now, go and get me some help.'

They turned and ran. In a few minutes they were battering on the door of number ten, Rectory Lane. After an agonising pause, Dorothy's father came to the door, wearing a coat over striped pyjamas.

'Daddy!' Dorothy flung herself at him. 'Someone's trying to kill us. They're in the churchyard with a gun.'

'What's all this?' said William, patting Dorothy's back. 'Take a breath, Dotty. You're safe now.'

'Mrs Kent, Mr Arthur's housekeeper, tried to kill us,' panted Justice. 'But Miss Robinson, our matron who's really a detective, saved us. They're both in the graveyard now. We escaped through a secret passage from Smugglers' Lodge.'

William blinked. John appeared, fully dressed, at his father's side.

'John,' said William, 'run for PC Hedges. You know where he lives, over the blacksmiths. I'm going to the graveyard.'

'We'll come with you,' said Justice.

'You stay here,' said William. He picked up a poker from the fireside and set off into the night.

CHAPTER 22

Dorothy's mother made them tea and wrapped them in blankets. How long ago had they and Mrs Kent left the kitchen in Smugglers' Lodge, in search of blankets? As if in answer, the cuckoo clock over the fireplace chirped twelve. Midnight. Elsie and Susan appeared on the stairs and were sent back to bed. Dorothy's mother, Hattie, sat with them on the sofa and waited.

Justice felt her eyes closing. She was in a tunnel, Sabre was with her but then he turned into a dragon and they flew high over the sea, the light in the tower was blinking at them and they saw Miss Robinson, in her nurse's uniform, riding on a sea-serpent . . .

A noise outside woke her with a start. William and John were coming back in, stamping in their heavy boots.

'Seems there's been some excitement up at the Lodge,' said William. 'PC Hedges has arrested the housekeeper and he's sent for reinforcements. Happen there's a private detective on the job too. I'm on my way to the Lodge now.'

'Can we come?' said Justice.

'No, dear,' said Dorothy's mother. 'You stay here, safely in the warm.'

'Please, Mum,' said Dorothy. 'We don't want to miss out on all the fun.'

John laughed and Hattie said, 'If you can call it fun, being chased by people with guns . . .'

'I reckon they'd better come,' said William. 'They're the only ones who know what's going on, seemingly. They can't come to any harm with me there.'

So Justice and Dorothy, wearing warm coats belonging to Hattie and John, followed William through the silent village. The rain had stopped and the storm had died down. The moon was shining over a silver sea. It seemed odd to think that they had just walked this same route, but underground.

When they got near to the Lodge they could hear Sabre barking. He sounded hoarse, as if he'd been barking for a long time. Justice directed William to the side door where he knocked loudly.

'Who is it?' came Miss Morris's voice.

'It's Justice,' shouted Justice.

The door opened and Miss Morris stood there, Sabre at her side, tail wagging. 'Justice! Dorothy! Wherever have you been? I've been worried sick about you. Mrs Kent seems to have locked us in. We've been trying to batter the door down.'

'It's a long story,' said Justice.

She had just finished telling it when Miss Robinson re-emerged, accompanied by PC Hedges and another officer. A grey-haired man who introduced himself as Detective Inspector Deacon said, 'Are you the lot from Highbury House? I've got men searching the marshes for you. Your headmistress is going crazy. She thinks that you've all fallen in the sea and been drowned.'

'Oh, dear,' said Miss Morris faintly. 'Can you get a message to her and let her know that we're safe?'

'I could if we had some of those new walkie-talkie things,' said DI Deacon. 'Wonderful, they are. Like carrying a telephone around with you. As it is . . . Hedges, get on your bike and take a message up to the school, will you?'

PC Hedges did not look delighted at the prospect but he saluted and left the room.

'Now,' said Deacon, 'we'd better have a look at the rest of the house. My guess is that we'll find the murder weapon in Mrs Kent's bedroom.'

The three policemen stomped out, followed by Dorothy's father. But Miss Robinson sat down at the kitchen table, for all the world as if she'd just popped in for a chat. The Highbury House crew stared at her, except for Alicia, who was asleep on the bench. Moira was still holding the rolling pin.

'Have the police arrested Mrs Kent?' said Justice.

'Yes,' said Miss Robinson. 'She hasn't confessed yet but I think she will when the police find the gun.'

'Are you really a private detective?' asked Rose.

'Yes.' Miss Robinson helped herself to the last piece of cake.

'Were you hired to find Mr Arthur's killer?' asked Miss Morris.

'Not at first,' said Miss Robinson, with a slight smile. 'Mr Arthur initially hired me to find his lost daughter. Then, when he was killed, I thought it was my duty to track down his murderer.'

Justice felt a slight pang at the thought that, when Mr Arthur had referred to employing a private detective, he'd meant Miss Robinson and not her. But then she thought that Mr Arthur *had* asked her to investigate. In a way, she'd been commissioned too.

'So you aren't really a nurse?' said Dorothy, with a glance at Justice.

'Technically, no,' said Miss Robinson. 'But I did serve in the ambulance corps during the war and I've got some basic medical knowledge. I didn't spot Ada's broken ankle though. I felt bad about that.'

'Did you find the missing daughter?' asked Stella. She'd run up to hug Justice when she first saw her and was now sitting close beside her friend.

'I have my suspicions,' said Miss Robinson. 'I found a letter addressed to "Bunny", which was Mr Arthur's pet name for her, but I must have dropped it somewhere.'

'You dropped it in the basement,' said Justice. 'I picked it up.' She turned to Miss Heron. 'You're Bunny, aren't you? That's why you were always so interested in Mr Arthur.'

'No,' said Miss Morris quietly. 'I am Mr Arthur's daughter.'

'You?' The second formers stared at their form mistress.

'Yes,' said Miss Morris. 'My name was originally Hildegarde but I changed it to Edna during the war. It didn't do to have a German name then. The Royal family did the same. Morris is my ex-husband's surname. I was briefly married and divorced. I'm still always called 'Miss' at school though.'

Justice remembered Mr Arthur describing his daughter as pretty, blonde and full of life. To her Miss Morris just looked like another teacher, with her little glasses and sensible clothes. Her hair was an indiscriminate colour that might be called blonde though. She remembered Dad saying that she'd always be his little girl, even when she was thirty-seven. She supposed that Mr Arthur had felt the same.

'I didn't know that Friedrich – Father – had even survived the war until I got the letter,' Miss Morris was saying. 'It was quite a shock.'

'Did you go to see him?' asked Justice. It suddenly seemed very important to know this.

'Yes,' said Miss Morris. 'I went through the tunnel so that no one knew where I was going. I came out into the study and he was there, sitting at his desk. He knew me as soon as I said his name.' She took out a handkerchief and held it to her eyes. 'I'm very glad that I met him as an adult, even if it was only once. Even if he couldn't see me. He was killed the next day.'

'He saw his solicitor that morning,' said Justice. 'Perkins told me. I bet Mr Arthur was going to change his will and leave everything to you. Before that, he was leaving the house to Mrs Kent. That's why she killed him.'

'I don't care about the will,' said Miss Morris. 'I'm just glad we were reconciled.'

'Did you see Mrs Kent when you came to the house?' asked Justice.

'No,' said Miss Morris. 'But Mr Arthur . . . Father . . . must have told her. He trusted her completely.' Her voice broke.

'I'm sorry.' Miss Heron put her hand on her colleague's arm. 'He was a wonderful man.' She turned to Justice. 'I'm not Mr Arthur's daughter, but I was a great admirer of his. He was one of the greatest marathon runners of all time. He won two Olympic medals.'

'I found them in his desk,' said Justice, 'when I was looking for clues.'

'You really have to stop snooping in people's private things,' said Miss Morris sternly.

'I wasn't snooping, I was sleuthing,' said Justice, though she was a bit hazy about the difference herself. She turned to Miss Robinson. 'Did you hit me over the head? That night when I followed you into the basement?'

'Yes,' said Miss Robinson. 'I felt bad about that too. But I had to stop you following me. I thought it could have been dangerous for you to find the secret passage. And I was right.'

'That's OK,' said Justice. 'Dorothy hit *you* over the head so I suppose we're even.'

'Was that you?' said Miss Robinson, turning to look at Dorothy. 'It was a good, hard blow. Well done.'

Dorothy blushed.

'Sabre knew that you were Mr Arthur's daughter,' said Justice to Miss Morris. 'He gave you his paw when you first met him, didn't he? And he wagged his tail when you came to the door earlier. He growled at Mrs Kent, which I thought was odd, because he must have known her well.'

'I met Sabre when I came through the tunnel,' said Miss Morris. 'He was sitting at Father's side. He's a highly intelligent animal. I'm going to take him back to the school with me. If I've inherited anything from my father, I'm glad it's him.'

'I expect you'll inherit the house too now,' said Miss Robinson. 'Especially if Mrs Kent is tried for murder.'

'I'm not sure I want it,' said Miss Morris. 'According to the locals this place has a dark past.'

Justice thought of Mr Arthur saying, '*Smugglers' Lodge is a house of secrets.*' She thought of the light shining in the tower and of Mr Arthur hoping it would light the way for lost travellers. She thought of the man with the cart warning them not to stray off the path. Then she thought of the skeleton in the tunnel and of the empty box beside it. Had the box once contained treasure? Was that why someone had died down there, on their way to the church and safety?

'I think I've found the smugglers' secret,' she said.

CHAPTER 23

And then, suddenly, the end of the Easter term was in sight. The weather became warm and sunny. The marshes were bright with yellow and purple flowers and the girls played rounders on the front lawn, Moira once hitting the ball so hard that it flew into the greenhouses with an almighty crash.

They performed *Alice in Wonderland* to an audience of staff and pupils. Rose was excellent as the White Rabbit but Helena as Alice forgot her lines several times, perhaps distracted by the presence of Monsieur Pierre in the front row. Justice worked like clockwork behind the scenes, making sure that everyone was in the right place and the right time, holding the right props. She got a special round of applause at the end. She felt as if she'd organised the whole thing herself. Was this what Miss de Vere meant when she said 'you see more from backstage'? Maybe this was what it was like to be a detective too. '*Assemble the facts and look for a pattern,*' said Mum's detective hero, Leslie Light. Sometimes you could only see the pattern if you stepped back a bit.

The play and the forthcoming holiday were all anyone could talk about but, amidst the excitement, there was the news that Miss Morris had suddenly acquired a dog. Sabre accompanied Hutchins on his evening rounds and was adored by all the girls. The competition to take him for walks was so fierce that Miss Morris had to draw up a rota. Miss Morris herself seemed unchanged. She was as strict as ever and showed no inclination to favour Justice because of their shared bond with Mr Arthur. One evening at prep, though, she took Justice aside and showed her a clipping from *The Times*. It said that Beryl Kent, 55, had pleaded guilty to the murder of Friedrich Arthur, 57. There was no mention of Mr Arthur's war record or of his Olympic medals.

'Is that all?' said Justice. It seemed so unfair that Mr Arthur's life should be reduced to a short paragraph in his favourite paper.

'It's up to us to keep his memory alive,' said Miss Morris. 'We won't forget him.'

Justice knew that she'd never forget Mr Arthur or the night when the cross-country team got lost in the fog. But, sometimes, when she was sitting in class or running round the playing field, it was hard to remember that she'd ever faced a woman with a pistol or followed an underground passage once used by smugglers. It was as if these adventures had happened to someone else.

Miss Hunting had been very excited by the discovery of the skeleton. She went into the tunnel herself to look at it, accompanied by PC Hedges and a woman archaeologist. To her disgust, Justice had not been allowed to go too. The archaeologist thought that the skeleton was about a hundred years old and had once been a man – 'Quite a tall one for the times,' said Miss Hunting. Was he a smuggler? Why had he died in the tunnel, so near to the iron rungs that led to safety? And what had been in the box? Treasure? Justice was a bit hazy as to what form this might have taken. Jewels? Gold coins? In books, pirates talked about 'pieces of eight' which, according to Miss Hunting, meant old Spanish dollars. But the box had been empty and the smuggler's secret had died with him.

Miss Robinson had left the school and was replaced by a temporary matron, a terrifyingly efficient woman who tried to make them all take cod-liver oil tablets at night. But, a few weeks after the events at Smugglers' Lodge, Justice received a small parcel. Inside was a brand-new torch and a note.

Dear Justice,
   I understand that you lost your torch in the tunnel so please accept this one as a replacement. A detective should never be without a light in the darkness.
   With very best wishes
   Maureen Robinson

Justice put the torch in her survival kit. She thought about Smugglers' Lodge and Mr Arthur hoping that its beacon would be a light in the darkness. She'd liked Miss Robinson, even though she had hit her over the head that time, and it had been exciting to meet a real private investigator. Justice was rather proud that Miss Robinson had called her a detective. She hoped that she'd have another crime to solve one day.

It turned out that Miss Heron *had* broken her arm but she was back taking games lessons in a few days, her arm in a sling. She was as keen on running as ever and announced that the cross-country competition would take place on the last day of term. 'That way, some of your parents can watch.' They were to compete against Roedean and two other girls' schools, St Margaret's and Totteridge Towers. Alicia's ankle was still painful so Stella was to be the fourth member of the team.

The last day of term was so busy, with all the packing and exchanging of addresses, that Justice kept forgetting about the race. When she remembered it was as if she had descended very fast in a lift. It was the first time that she had taken part in any sort of competition and she didn't want to let herself down – or Dad, or Miss Heron. And, though she would never admit it, she didn't want to let Highbury House down either.

'I'm so nervous,' she said to Stella. 'I think I've forgotten how to put one foot in front of the other.'

'You'll be fine,' said Stella. 'You're always out in front with Moira. I'll be right at the back.'

Justice looked at her overnight case, which was open on the bed. The brass dog from Mr Arthur was sitting on top of her folded dressing gown. She held it out to Stella. 'Pat him for luck,' she said. 'After all, Mr Arthur did win two Olympic medals.'

Stella smiled and patted the dog's shiny head. 'Bring us luck, Mr Arthur,' she said.

*　　*　　*

'Remember,' said Miss Heron, when they gathered in the changing room before the race, 'it's a team competition. Only the first ten runners get points so the winning school will be the one that has the most girls in the top ten. The first placed competitor gets sixteen points, the second fifteen, and so on. Watch out for each other and keep an eye on the placing. Ivy Robin and Jennifer Fortescue from Roedean are very talented runners, they've won quite a few competitions already. We've got to try to prevent them from coming first and second. I've heard that Penny Meaker from Totteridge Towers is good too.' She smiled. 'But I'm sure we are the strongest team overall. The others have weak links. We haven't. You should all be capable of top ten finishes. Moira and Justice could make the top five. And, most of all, enjoy it. Remember, you are blazing a trail for female distance runners to come.'

Miss Heron looked so fierce, standing there in her divided skirt and aertex top, her arm in a sling, that Justice felt that, if their teacher's willpower alone could produce results, she *would* get in the top five. But, when they walked out on to the field and saw the other teams, Justice felt her confidence sinking. The other girls all looked much bigger and stronger, wearing professional-looking running clothes and determined expressions. Miss Heron shook hands with the visiting teachers, all of whom were grey-haired and solidly built. Justice couldn't imagine them going on evening runs with their teams. The girls shook hands too. Ivy from Roedean smiled at Justice and Justice suddenly liked her. The other runners were grim-faced, jostling for position at the start line.

The whole school seemed to have gathered around the gymnasium to watch them – from the first years through to the sixth formers, parents and teachers too. Justice saw Miss Morris with Sabre, Monsieur Pierre in a panama hat, Helena Bliss, her hair loose, trying to look like a Hollywood star, Dorothy waving from the steps and – oh, hooray! – there was Dad, standing next to Miss de Vere, taller than anyone else around him, waving and smiling. Justice waved back and suddenly felt capable of anything.

Miss Heron blew her whistle and the race started. In the excitement Justice started too fast and had to force herself to hold back and follow her game plan. She could see Rose's blonde ponytail ahead of her with Moira's red head at her side. Stella was next to Justice, matching her stride for stride. As they ran down the hill towards the spinney, some of the runners were already tiring. But Justice and Stella had the advantage of knowing the route. They jogged onwards, the ground now dry and powdery beneath their feet. As they passed the tower, Justice thought of all the late-night adventures she'd had at Highbury House, the time when she'd gone to the tower at midnight, the time when she'd been locked in there with Dorothy, the night at Smugglers' Lodge, the escape through the tunnel and the mad race through the graveyard. Today, though, they faded into the background. The race was all that mattered.

Around the tower and up the hill. Justice and Stella passed a few more runners who had started too fast and were now struggling. The leaders had almost reached the gymnasium. Justice could see Ivy out in front, followed by Rose, Moira and another girl she didn't recognise. Then there was another group of four, then Justice and Stella. They were just in the top ten but there was a long way to go.

As they passed the gymnasium, the roar of the crowd was quite deafening. Justice even imagined that she could hear Dad's voice, and Dorothy's, amid the general noise. She quickened her pace, buoyed up by the support but, as they started down the hill towards the tower, she felt the beginnings of a stitch, a stabbing pain in her side. She tried not to think about it, controlling her breath as Miss Heron had taught her. She had to do well, in front of all her schoolmates and teachers, in front of Dad. Amazingly, after a few hundred yards, the ache seemed to go away – or maybe

Justice just didn't notice it any more. As they rounded the tower for the second time, Justice drew ahead of Stella. There were only five other runners in front of her now. Rose had fallen back and Ivy, Moira and two other girls were pulling ahead. She thought the two other runners were Jennifer Fortescue from Roedean and Penny Meaker from Totteridge Towers. There should be another Highbury House runner in the top five. Justice tried to force her heavy legs to go faster. Halfway up the final hill she passed Rose, still running valiantly but swaying slightly as if she was exhausted.

'Go on, Justice!' panted Rose. 'Go for it!'

Justice felt as if Rose's words had propelled her forwards. She thought of Mr Arthur saying, *'You mustn't measure everything by Rose'* but now Rose was on her side, willing her to do well. She thought of Miss Heron saying, *'It's not about being good at games, it's about being determined.'* She thought of Mr Arthur: *'Remember, you are a detective and detectives never give up.'* She could hear the crowd yelling and thought of her father cheering her on. *'Veritas et fortitudo,'* that's what he always said. Truth and courage. She put her head down and tried to summon a last burst of speed.

She passed Penny Meaker and then, suddenly, she was level with Moira and Jennifer. Moira looked tired – Justice could see what an effort it was for her to keep going, but Jennifer was pulling ahead, grimacing in determination. 'Go on, Justice,' gasped Moira, just as Rose had done. Justice thought of Moira brandishing a rolling pin in the kitchen of Smugglers' Lodge; of the five of them running along the coastal path in the mist. There were only a few more yards to go. Ivy had already finished. Justice's legs were on fire and her heart seemed to have risen up into her throat. But she dug down and, from somewhere, she found a sprint that carried her past Jennifer and over the line in second place.

Justice collapsed on the grass. She heard Miss Heron saying, 'Well done, Justice. You did it!' but the blood was singing in her ears and it was hard to take anything in. She saw Jennifer cross the line, closely followed by Moira, then Penny Meaker with Rose, summoning a final burst of speed, hot on her heels, then a Roedean girl and Stella, neck and neck. A St Margaret's runner came next, then another Roedean girl and then there was a long wait while the remaining runners struggled up the hill. The Highbury House Cross-country Team stood together, leaning on each other's shoulders, trying to get their breath back.

'What's the final score?' said Moira. 'I think we were all in the top ten but so were all the Roedean team.'

'Miss Heron and the other teachers are trying to work it out,' said Stella.

They approached the gymnasium and saw Miss Heron and the other games teachers in a huddle. Miss de Vere was there too, a megaphone in her hand. There was also a bespectacled man who had been introduced earlier as the race umpire. Miss Heron handed him a piece of paper, he studied it and then passed it to Miss de Vere. She raised the megaphone.

'I have the results of the cross-country competition,' she announced, her amplified voice echoing against the brick walls of the gymnasium. Justice, Stella, Moira and Rose all held hands.

'Congratulations to all the competitors on a really splendid race,' said Miss de Vere. The last word reverberated around them. Race, ace, ace.

'The results are: St Margaret's, eight points.'

Scattered applause.

'Totteridge Towers, thirteen points.'

More applause. Rose was squeezing Justice's hand so tightly that she wondered if it would ever be the same again.

'Roedean, forty-seven points.'

Loud applause. It was such a huge score that it was a few

seconds before Justice realised that Roedean were in second place, which must mean . . .

'And the winning team is Highbury House, with forty-eight points.'

The girls went mad, cheering, whooping and hugging each other. Miss Heron came running over, clapping them on their backs.

'Well done, team! Only one point in it. So, if Justice hadn't made that final sprint . . .'

'You did it, Justice!' Stella hugged her again.

'We all did it,' said Justice. She felt as if she had left her body and was floating high in the blue, April sky. In a haze, she saw Dad coming towards her.

'Congratulations, Justice.' He hugged her tightly. 'Congratulations, all of you. A fine team performance.'

The other parents were gathering round. Rose's mother, elegant in a pink two-piece; Stella's mother grinning widely, a child attached to each hand; Moira's parents, both red-haired, her father wearing a kilt. 'Well done, Justice!' shouted a deep voice and Justice saw Dorothy's parents, with John grinning beside them. She took her dad over to meet them. Dorothy's mum gave her a lovely hug and John said, 'Not bad for a girl.'

'I'll race you one day,' said Justice.

Miss de Vere walked over to join them. 'Congratulations, Justice,' she said. 'A really splendid race.'

'Thank you,' said Justice. But Miss de Vere had already turned towards Justice's dad.

'I hope you're proud of your daughter, Herbert.'

'I certainly am, Dolores.'

Herbert? Dolores? What was going on? But before Justice could say anything, Rose and Moira rushed up to her.

'The results are up!' They grabbed a hand each and the three of them galloped over to the gymnasium, where the list was pinned on the door. Stella and Moira were already there, Stella holding her little sister in her arms.

There it was in black-and-white:

1. Ivy Robin, Roedean   16 points
2. Justice Jones, Highbury House   15 points
3. Jennifer Fortescue, Roedean   14 points
4. Moira Campbell, Highbury House   13 points
5. Penny Meaker, Totteridge Towers   12 points
6. Rose Trevellian-Hayes, Highbury House   11 points
7. Lucy-Anne Mullins, Roedean   10 points
8. Stella Goldman, Highbury House   9 points
9. Bella Mancini, St Margaret's   8 points
10. Yvonne Hope, Roedean   7 points

1st place. Highbury House: *48* points
2nd place. Roedean: *47* points
3rd place. Totteridge Towers: *12* points
4th place. St Margaret's: *8* points

Justice walked back to the school, arm in arm with her father. She had a medal round her neck. It wasn't quite an Olympic gold but she had to admit that it felt pretty good all the same.

'You were brilliant,' said Herbert. 'What a finish. I didn't know you were such a good runner.'

'Nor did I,' said Justice. 'It was Miss Heron really. She believed that I could do it and so I did it.'

'Miss de Vere tells me that you've been having another exciting term,' said Herbert, 'catching another murderer.'

'You know all about that,' said Justice. 'I wrote and told you.'

'I didn't know that it involved a secret passage, a private detective and a dangerous armed criminal.'

'I was saving that to tell you in the hols,' said Justice. 'I wanted to make a good story of it.'

'It is a good story,' said her dad, 'but it's rather an alarming one.'

'Well, you were the one who told me to keep an eye on Miss Robinson,' said Justice. 'Why was that? Was Miss de

Vere suspicious of her? Is that why she wanted to talk to you on the half holiday?'

'Yes,' said Herbert. 'Amongst other things. Dolores . . . Miss de Vere was starting to think that the new matron wasn't quite what she claimed to be. She asked me if I'd come across anyone of her description in the course of my work. I hadn't – but now I think she must be the private detective that some of my solicitors use. Her nickname's Florence Nightingale because she often disguises herself as a nurse.'

'I liked her,' said Justice. 'She sent me a new torch.'

'Well, I hope you won't use it to go into any more underground tunnels,' said her dad. 'Do try not to get into any more danger next term.'

'I won't,' said Justice. 'School's very dull most of the time.'

But, as they approached the red-brick house, golden in the sunlight, she found that she was almost looking forward to the summer term.

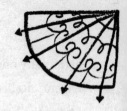

Acknowledgements

The Justice books are inspired by my mum, Sheila, who went to boarding school in the 1930s. Sheila's father was an actor, not a lawyer, but in many respects I think she was very like Justice. Sheila loved detective stories but, unlike Justice, was never lucky enough to find a dead body in her school. Highbury House is completely imaginary, as are all the characters in this book. The one exception is Ivy Robin, ex-Roedean pupil and champion athlete, who appears as an early version of herself.

Books are team efforts and I'd like to thank everyone at Hachette Children's for their faith in me and hard work on my behalf, especially my fabulous editor, Sarah Lambert, whose wise suggestions have made this book so much better and Dom Kingston, publicist extraordinaire and the best company on tour. Huge thanks, as always, to my wonderful agent, Rebecca Carter, who has believed in these books from the beginning.

Thanks to Alison Padley for the cover design and to Nan Lawson for the fabulous illustration. When she was at school, my mum used to write stories about a girl spy called Nan Lawes. I like to think that the similarity in names is not a coincidence.

Love and thanks always to my husband Andrew and our children, Alex and Juliet. This book is for Gabriella and Rafael, Sheila's great-grandchildren.

And finally, thanks to you and to everyone who has read and enjoyed these books. Your support means everything to me.

Elly Griffiths
2020

Look out for Justice's
first adventure!

**Missing maids, suspicious teachers and
a snow storm to die for ...**

For a fearless girl called Justice Jones, super-smart
super-sleuth, it's just the start of her spine-tingling
adventures at Highbury House Boarding School.

*'Splendidly moody and twisty,
like Malory Towers but with added corpses ...'*
Financial Times

HIGHBURY HOUSE